Las Vegas
on
Twelve Dollars a Day

D1232873

By COL Mike Bennett

Nearing retirement, an independent contractor enabling CIA technical operations mentors the next generation of patriots in their craft until tragedy pulls him back into the game to rollback China's global ambitions.

Jon Prescott had made mistakes in his life, as most people do, but there were some decisions he had made in his past he wanted to rectify. Following 9/11, he started a journey along a path toward redemption, a path that would lead him to the vast stretches of federal lands out west where he would train the next generation of special operators and technical intelligence officers. These young American men and women are fighting to preserve the liberties that America offers and would soon join the fray to flush terrorist strongholds out of East Africa. Although the Tier 1 operators rightfully claim the mantle of leadership in the realms requiring violence of action, the technical enablers of low-vis operations tend to their duty's unseen in the shadows.

In appreciation, this book is dedicated not only to the special operations community who stand in the breech, but to those enablers on the fringe, unseen and unheard.

Proceeds from the profits from sales will be donated to the Special Operations Warriors Foundation whose purpose is to ensure 'every child of a fallen SOF warrior receives a college education.' If you, too, wish to give: make checks payable to SOWF and mail to -- PO Box 89367, Tampa, FL 33689

Their website is: https://specialops.org/

To reduce costs, each image inside the paperback version is in black and white. For those who wish to see the images in color and expand the images to see greater detail, go to my Facebook page, "Mike Bennett, Colonel".

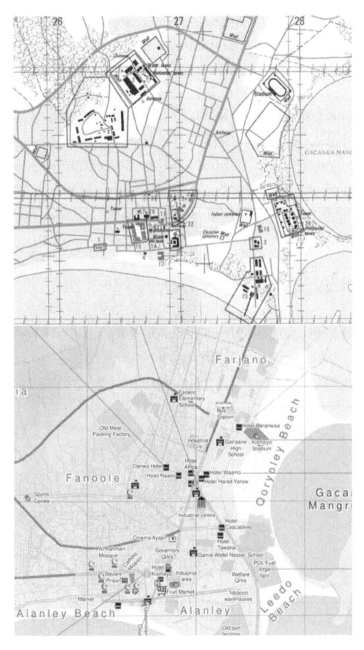

Kismaayo, Somalia

Table of Contents

Chapter 1
2007-2008, Syria

The web spanning the Middle East and beyond was centuries in the making. Not a web of gossamer silk, but one of malice anchored by conviction, with its center point being Tehran and many radii along each axis of opportunity. This was not a web of wonderous symmetry that artfully caught the sun kissing a sprinkle of glistening dew drops on a pristine spring morning. No, its core of expanding boundaries was a tangled cobweb in the shape of a crescent joining Lebanon, Syria, Bahrain, Iraq, Iran, Azerbaijan, Yemen, and western Afghanistan.. Within its dark recesses was not Shelob, but a man. A man who sought to sow the seeds of discontent, pollinate the fervor of the adherents of Shia Islamist ideology and reap its bloody harvest under the guise of the tenets of the Cultural Revolution.

Qasem Soleimani was not yet at the height of his powers, but well on his way. As the commander of the Iranian Revolutionary Guard Corps – Quds Force, it would be a courtesy to define his role as exporting mischief to influence and fund miscreants ranging from the Islamic Jihad to Lebanese Hezbollah. Such euphemistic characterizations would only be irresponsible. Plain and simple, he was a killer, and he was a hater, but his skills to knit together a blooming network of chaos were to be respected. He was a master strategist and fearsome opponent who devised alliances that prosecuted layers of operations nested within operations with an alacrity that was awesome to behold.

The Americans were a problem. Saddam Hussein was a problem, too, but with him removed, Iraq was less manageable in a bid for hegemonic regional dominance. There were other vectors to explore such as Yemen or Somalia, but Soleimani had to devise something to thwart Bush's plans and he knew exactly to whom to commission this task and how best to achieve the desired result.

Explosively Formed Penetrators (EFPs) were high explosives packed into a cylinder akin to a paint can with the lid removed. A concave liner of professionally milled copper or steel is then clamped over the cylinder's open end. When the explosive is detonated, it creates a focused jet of hypervelocity molten metal that can cut through even the heaviest main battle tank armor at close range. These were coupled with passive infrared sensors (used to initiate a device as vehicles pass) and numerous radio-controlled arming switches to turn on the sensors.

The IRGC sought to preposition EFPs in Abu Kamal as well as train local Iraqi or Syrian Shiites to mass produce EFPs. The Al Bukumal workshop included an industrial press that used specialized dies to make EFP liners. A range of EFP inventory was amassed as well, with diameters of six, eight, and twelve inches, matching the variety of dies that were provided. High-quality copper liners were accumulated alongside less effective steel ones. The press and other large equipment had been installed in a concealed basement, a major logistical undertaking. These EFPs and trainers could enable Shiite militants along the Euphrates to keep armored vehicles out of key towns, making mini-uprisings much more practical if Iran wished to foment such incidents.

Leading this cell was a cadre of QF lower-tier commanders: Qais Qazali, the leader of the Qazali Network; Azhar al Dulaimi, one of Qazali's senior tactical commanders; and Iraqi Shiite group Kataib Hezbollah leader Jamal Madan al-Tamimi. It was known that al-Tamimi provided EFP training at a camp in Iraq and "offered logistical and financial support" to smuggle the EFPs along the Al Qaim/Abu Kamal ratline. This trio of malcontents consolidated their manufactured 'product' under the guise of an electronic repair shop in the Midhat Pasha Souq in Al-Rawda Square. For many months they plied their deadly trade, but they did not go unnoticed for long.

On the evening of the 27th of October 2008, a fleet of helicopters carried operators from A Squadron, SFOD-D across the Iraq-Syria border area of Abu Kamal. Their target was a building site situated at the village of Sukkariyeh that was suspected of being the base of operations for Qais Qazali who was responsible for smuggling large quantities of guns, money, and terrorists into Iraq. The plan was to swoop in quickly, snatch Qazali, then make a quick exit in as stealthy and discrete manner as possible unless fired upon. The emphasis was on capture, not kill, as the intent was to interrogate Qazali to learn more about the origins of the EFP network.

Qazali's deputy, **Azhar al Dulaimi**, quite uncharacteristically had a lull in discipline while riding in a white Bongo as SIGINT assets geolocated his cellphone. A Pred in orbit over the border was vectored into the area to perform a vehicle follow on the white Bongo and then fix the target. As is often the case with high-risk special ops, not everything went to plan. The Little Birds came under ground fire as they approached their insertion points. The Deltas were inserted onto the ground by

8

teams of 4 while 2 DAPs provided covering fire. A fierce gun battle raged as the site's defenders were engaged from both the ground and air until no more resistance was met. During the battle Qazali was killed and his body taken back to Iraq to confirm his DNA.

Due more to luck than skill, one squirter had escaped. The terrorist al-Tamimi would live to fight another day.

Chapter 2

2001-2002, Idaho National Laboratory (INL)

The world had changed.

Jon Prescott had been working at an offsite in Chantilly, Virginia when he walked past the glassed-in conference room called 'the fishbowl'. He saw a group of colleagues standing around the TV which was odd for normally obsessive law enforcement professionals that ran the electronic surveillance program for the FBI.

Quite literally, as he walked in and saw a black plume of smoke streaming out of what appeared to be one of the twin towers in NYC, a second commercial airliner slammed into the adjacent building. Every adult alive remembers that day. It was the day when Jon put past feelings aside and made a promise to himself, he would reengage and get back into the game.

His initial role was as a trainer and mentor of the next generation of technical intelligence collectors, and he performed this task as an independent contractor for CIA. He was part of a small cadre that devised a finishing course for individuals who, having already passed arduous selection processes and follow-on training courses, were emerging from that pipeline and ready to deploy to dangerous environments overseas.

The program of instruction he had devised was basic in its technical nature but would require the application of nearly perfect tradecraft to succeed. In other words, the emphasis was on the more arcane skills of espionage conducted in a hostile and clandestine environment, not cutting-edge technology. His 'students' were already operating under various covers, and he would likely never know their true names. They travelled to Idaho Falls Regional Airport under an alias then reported into the security badge office at the Willow Creek Building (WCB) to procure the necessary access badges to specific areas of the massive complex.

This POI was oriented to season a 'husband/wife' team that would operate as a singleton pair and be given taskings and pass reporting through a case officer while overseas. The premise was tried and true: they could perform their duties under far less suspicion than a solitary man trying to blend in amongst a foreign backdrop. Jon would play two roles—first, as primary one-on-one instructor, and second, as the handler providing tasking. In classroom mode, the pair would address him by his call sign, Serpico, but in the public, they would call him Jon. Each iteration of this POI was tailored to the pairs to be assessed that were from entities across the IC, specifically from the Joint Reconnaissance Task Force. The JRTF was a waived, unacknowledged special access program comprised of persons detailed from DOD and national intelligence agencies. JRTF had an extrajudicial charter loosely organized around Title 10 and 50 authorities and was tailored to satisfy intelligence requirements beyond even the covert activities over which Congress had oversight. Outside of its Crystal City offices, JRTF was known only as 'the firm'.

Jon met his newlyweds at WCB with a single, curt comment, "You didn't do an SDR. Meet me in room 327 of the Hilton Garden Inn at 8pm tonight. Hi, I'm Jon and you were both on the clock when you stepped on the tarmac. See you at 8."

An SDR was a surveillance detection route—a circuitous but deliberate and logically explainable path from point to point with the objective of being able to discern if you were being followed. Kim and Jason Taylor's behavior was fairly typical—each pair that came through course, regardless of location or background, assumed that they had already gone through exhaustive vetting and gut checks, and that this was merely a check the block to their actual assignment. In this line of business, an assumption like that can mean mission failure.

Still, these were professionals with skillsets and mindsets that required little correction to get back on course. Jon respected their abilities and dedication and knew he didn't have to come down on them like a ton of bricks, the point had been made and likely taken with corresponding gravity. At 8:01pm, well within the 4-minute window, he heard a knock on the door.

He rose from his chair, undid the security latch, and opened the door, "Hey, ya'll, come on in."

Jason walked in and shook his hand as did Kim. Jon said, "Jason, you should always let your wife precede you when greeting an old friend. Welcome. I'd like you both to relax, come and have a seat and I'll give you a quick rundown of the next few weeks."

Kim blushed a bit and remarked, "We both have been trained to work in larger teams or alone, but I've never been married before!"

Jon nodded and proceeded with his well-rehearsed spiel, "Understandable. That's why you are here. I know the firm never briefs you in any detail on training scenarios, and that is the point. Improvise, adapt. Until we get to the facilities on campus, I'll only skim over the top of the scenario, but for now I'd like you both to just get accustomed to your new roles.

My role is only to guide you as best I can. This is a Master's level curriculum—I don't know your full backgrounds and I don't need to. I may cover ground you have already touched upon from your previous organizations and in some ways this onboarding process will bore you, but it is merely to refine your undergrad skills and adapt them as a married couple."

Jason's had an intense look, and Jon suspected that he was a full-blown type A personality when he blurted, "Great! When do we get started?"

Jon grinned and said, "You mustn't have been listening, you already have! Consider yourselves to be at an intermediate staging base, an ISB. For now, enjoy a relaxing evening. I have tickets to the Colonial Theatre, if you hurry, you can get there in time for the opening curtain call. Here is your room keycard; you are right next door. It's nice to meet you both, but I do need some shuteye. We'll meet downstairs by the fireplace and ready to checkout at 7:30 for breakfast. Goodnight."

Once again, right on time, 7:32am by Jon's watch, the couple entered the lounge area looking refreshed, but not fully comfortable, a bit on edge. Jon was fully switched on when they sat down, and a bit brusque in stating, "You two did not make love last night. Don't say anything, just listen. You are a young couple, and you should act that way. You walked hand in hand along the Greenbelt Trail, and that's good, that's consistent, but you'll have to extend the act beyond public eyes. You could be monitored, and Americans often are by professional

13

counterintelligence services in many different countries. Just keep that in mind, you are always being watched. Not a lot of time this morning. Here are your tickets; you'll take a short hop to the Rexburg-Madison County Airport just north of Test Area North on campus. It's up to you as how you get to SMC. Join me in classroom 6 at 6pm."

"Hey, folks, how was the trip?", Jon beamed.

Jason replied, "bumpy, bumpy—we flew in a tiny plane through a thunderstorm." Kim nodded greenly and with little enthusiasm.

"So," Jon began, "tell me about your trip. I know ya'll did a cover stop at the Museum of Idaho, good. Kim, can you estimate the rate of flow and width of the Snake River along the Greenbelt trail?"

Kim stammered, "No, sir."

Jon corrected, "Other than perhaps showing deference to my obvious relatively advanced age, try not to use anything like military jargon or mannerisms, it's not cover consistent unless for some reason you two might deploy as a married couple like Defense attaches. Jason, any observations about the destination airport and brief me how you two got here. Any hang-ups?"

Jason leapt at the chance to shine, "The location of the airport at night is lit by a rotating beacon that projects two beams of light, one white and one green, 180 degrees apart. It's a single runway equipped with runway end identifier lights (REILs). We took the Rexburg Park and Ride bus out of Lane 4 and down Rt. 512 through guard gate 676 to SMC."

Jon enthused, "Excellent report. Succinct, accurate. Did you notice anything else about the airport facilities, how many hangars, orientation of the runway, that sort of thing?"

Visibly deflated, Jason murmured, "No. I didn't."

Jon parried, "Kim? Your thoughts?"

Kim added, "When we landed, we were headed straight into the setting sun and I only saw 2 hangars."

Jon praised, "Not bad, you two. It's a start. Without specific tasking to sensitize you to requirements, not bad at all. Plenty of room for improvement, but that is why you are here. Let me tell you a bit about the exercise scenario—it is nothing new, we are using the general outline of the Q-course. You have infilled Pineland, a communist regime backwater dominated by Sunni Islamic fundamentalists in a mountainous or high-desert plain sitting astride massive gas and oil reserves and singularly hostile to Israel with the requisite Death to America nonsense. The host nation regime security forces wear a black and tan uniform with a leather Sam Browne belt and Makarovs and drive white Land Rovers with the Southern Pineland Security Company (SPSC) logo on the doors. We are supporting an insurgent force with intelligence and logistics.

Your role in all this is to clandestinely supply that intel through a case officer, in this case, me. Operationally, you have no interaction with any other special operations forces supporting the insurgents or the auxiliary, your only conduit for pushing or pulling information is me. I will interface with the G-chief to determine what he needs and to advise him what collection abilities we can bring to bear to advance his objectives.

Although we are doing the textbook UW thing, this C.O./ operative relationship will be your bread and butter as the mechanics are similar enough. The key take away is this: it's a high threat, high risk, but hopefully high payoff environment as far as US foreign policy goes. You will plan and conduct operational acts, live in a low-profile manner and live your cover. Questions so far?"

Kim and Jason nodded in unison.

"Over the course of the next few weeks, we'll concentrate on some specific skills and equipment you'll use at your assignment," Jon continued. "I am going to jump right in with some SIGINT theory to help you decide what tool to use to solve opportunities as they arise. Idaho National Lab has several types of fully working or replicated networks, but in this case I have been instructed to bring you up to speed on the GSM 2G network because that is what is most prevalent in your follow on assignment. The technical training here at INL is meant to serve as a rehearsal of your target environment."

Jon winced a bit and said, "I apologize for the power point slides, but I'll make this very brief. Also, you will be issued a laptop that you'll be able to get through any security checkpoint. You don't have to take notes unless you want to. The notes will stay here and be destroyed when you leave. On a concealed partition of the flash drive and encapsulated further by an encryption program called TrueCrypt, you'll have access to some of the specific channel release messaging protocols and UNIX commands to operate applications like RAMORA for demodulation and that sort of thing. So, I'll dive right into some theory."

He flipped on his first slide:

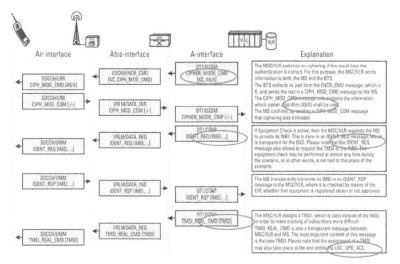

Jon took a deep breath. "Busy slide, but there are three attack points of interest, each with their own advantages or disadvantages. The A-interface greatest advantage is that at this point, the voice is unencrypted. This is often denoted by A5/X. At points forward, on the Abis and the Air-interface, it IS encrypted, leading to a whole lot of other gear. On the A-interface, there are some subscriber or target identifying codes such as the IMEI which identifies the specific cell phone or device. The TMSI is a temporary identifier rendered by the network but can work in a pinch when the IMEI is not available. On the A-interface, messages to initiate locating are called out by the LOC_UPD_ACC parameter, the value here is its immediacy but the detractor is a lack of targetable fidelity. We tracking?"

Kim offered, "But these are going to require access to actual facilities. Why not circumvent that by exploiting the Um interface?" Jason sat uncharacteristically quiet with a glazed look on his face.

Jon laughed, "Careful what you reveal, Kim. I see that you two were paired to complement each other's qualities. That in itself is worth noting and discussing—you two are a team now, and you'll get to know each other's strengths and weakness over time and how best to apply those attributes. Remember that! Kim, you are right, but for now, we just want to focus on solving problems and taking opportunities as they avail themselves, so I'll press on with the Abis-interface on the next slide, and this will be brief."

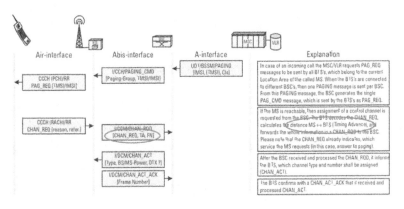

Jon continued, "The Abis is all about the Timing Advance or TA – this is a means to calculate the distance between facilities. Since the facilities are known, immovable points, with the right algorithms and software, you can plot where multiple timing advance arcs intersect. That is the advantage of the Abis-location, location, location. Also, the Abis-interface in some situations is transmitted over the air on a microwave link, so it can be intercepted like the Um interface like Kim already mentioned.

For the purpose of A-interface intercept, you'll train on an Tektronix commercial protocol analyzer. You'll work out of an MSC mockup here on campus. For that block of instruction, Felix will be your technician.

For the Abis, you'll use a company called G-Systems wireline gear that is purpose designed for 2G networks in the Sandbox. For wireless systems with parabolic antenna, you'll learn processor applications such as RAMORA or HAFLEX for demodulation, as well as familiarization to the some of the other tools such as TAROTCARD. Janice will be your instructor for both the BSC mockup or on the PCM gear at tower 2.

The Um or air-interface is probably your best bet, on that you are correct, Kim, because I'd say there is a much higher probability you can get access via the equipment available. But it truly is meant to be used when in the Finish portion of the Find, Fix and Finish loop. You will train on a system called TYPHON which is standard NSA gear. It is essentially unattributable when you break it down—all the components are sanitized. But there is one distinct disadvantage—the TYPHON works only by mimicking a real cell tower. It sends out a stronger signal to the mobile subscriber device, the cell phone, and that is how it gets the timing advance data. At the same time, the real network is alerted to what it perceives as a dropped call and now people versus machines get involved to make inquiries. Plus, it doesn't get call content, so it is used only sparingly. Arthur will train you on TYPHON and read you on to a program called RADIANT GEMSTONE."

Kim was clearly stoked, Jason, not so much. Jon finished, "That's it for today. I'd advise you two do some area familiarization and scout the general area. Felix will meet you at Building 109 at 8'oclock in the morning. Your pantry is stocked for now; here are your keys and your welcome packet with all the rules and a map. Page me, yes, you heard me correctly, page me at *3976* if you need me. I'll see you tomorrow in the mess hall at lunchtime. Felix will let me know when he is finished."

Chapter 3

2002, Idaho National Laboratory

Kim and Jason had met with Jon for a quick working lunch in which further ground rules were drawn. Even though inside classroom environments were to be treated as 'administrative' and not 'tactical', henceforth, no matter whether in Pineland or outside its border, any meeting with a CO would be treated as a personal meeting (PM), and the normal security protocols like an SDR applied. If a PM were needed, the pair would case the area of the meet, submit a casing report, and adjust accordingly. Jon showed them an additional hidden application on the laptop for covert communications (COVCOM), issued each of them an old school Skytel satellite 2-way text pager and given them keys to their transport.

Their transport was a 1994 Mitsubishi Montero with right-hand drive and a stick shift. Only Kim had driven a stick shift before, but never sat in a right-side driver seat with the shift lever to her left. Thankfully, the foot pedal order was the same, but she was rusty driving the stick and stalled the car several times at stop signs. The only thing modern in the vehicle was a very large, in-console Sirius radio set. They thought that was pretty odd, considering how abused the Montero was in other regards. Also, they were informed that scheduled evolutions or the general plan of the day would be posted on a white board on their refrigerator. Jon's last cryptic instruction was, "Don't be late. Don't be light."

The pair spent a long afternoon with Janice learning the G-box and gear related to intercepting Pulse Code Modulation (PCM) links accounting for Schur Recursion of the RPELTP encoder and other fascination tidbits of the 3GPP specifications. The theory pieces of the instruction were a little too technical, even for Kim, so they both focused on the equipment and the fact that only through mastery of the gear would their efforts be meaningful. When they returned to their apartment, a note on the white board specified: 'Meet Jon tomorrow at Track 5 at 10:00am, uniform—Roughs'.

After consulting their welcome packet map, they spent the evening conducting a route reconnaissance to the training site called 'Track 5' in their welcome packet. Test Area North (TAN) of INL is comprised of vast desert-lava rolling hill terrain with views of the Teton mountains each peak easily discernable to the far away eastern horizon. TAN has numbered test facilities dotted throughout the campus (TAN-646, TAN-650, TMI-2, etc.) with standard, cinder block structures denoting the seriousness of the 1950's nuclear programs from which they were funded. After dozens of kilometers of straight as an arrow rough asphalt paving leading through the definition of the middle of nowhere, what looked like an abandoned Middle Eastern village complete with minaret appeared on their right 6 kilometers from their destination, a replica of the BSR Advanced Driving Training Site, aka 'Track 5'.

They returned to their apartment, exhausted. To keep appearances of normality, they played some moderately romantic music at a respectful volume, while one made a quick stir fry and the other typed up the laborious report on the 'special' laptop.

The next day, Jon waited in the parking lot. At 9:59am, the pair strolled up wearing 6-pocket pants, plaid Prana tops and Vasque low tops. Kim was the first to speak, "Good morning, Jon."

Jon offered, "Morning. A little change of pace today. The technical crew tell me you are doing well with the hands-on training; that's really what is important. You are going to have several days of the hands-on, but to break it up there is a whole lot else to cover. I see that you went though the village, good spot for an SDR or a cover stop. I want you to continue that practice each time we come out this way and familiarize yourself with the layout. You probably figured out by now, and noticed some oddities, but it's an approximate replica of where your follow-on assignment is.

It's general layout will be augmented by the engineers with more specific detail as we progress through the POI. It's streets and buildings will become more populated as we ramp up. At the end of a training day that you pass through the Ville, you will draw a strip map of your route and observations. Place your map in a concealment device I provide, and you'll then place that CD at a cache location I have already cased. We tracking?"

Kim and Jason both nodded. Cache sites and some of the other traditional forms of tradecraft were very familiar to them from their past assignments. Jason noticed that Jon was similarly dressed in outdoor gear attire.

"Fair enough," Jon continued. "Welcome to Track 5. You'll have a lot of fun here—all this, and a paycheck, too. On this complex, we have three high-speed and one specialized paved road circuit each with dedicated skid pads and six kilometers of multiple unimproved road circuits. You will each drive the Montero through different timed events, and from here on out, on all roads here on the INL campus, you will drive on the right side of road, as will any other traffic you encounter.

You'll be shown a modified TYPHON-type receiver that's been concealed under the center console as has the antenna been adapted to the roof rack. Same operating principals as you have seen, but Arthur will meet you here after you've had a few more days on the baseline gear and then he'll brief you on the truck's gear.

On the BSR complex, there are three configurable, multi-story Close Quarter Battle (CQB) facilities, but you two are going to focus more on ridiculously discrete concealed carry and 2-meter shooting. For all this training at Track 5, Jack is your man. I warn you—Jack is a fucking madman, and he will expect your 100% attention and 110% concentration. I pray you don't, I really do, but if you have to use any of this, it's because your life is at risk. For each Track 5 evolution, I will meet you right here and lead you thru the O-course or a road march. Follow me."

Jason kind of smirked when Jon turned away and sauntered off towards a gray metal maintenance bay with assorted BendPak hydraulic car lifts, overhead heavy-duty electric wire rope hoists and large wheeled tool boxes that obviously comprised the garage and staff to keep the large fleet of various aging behemoths in running condition. This guy must be pushing 40, he's gonna lead ME on a road march?? There was some greasy looking dude by a lift in a patched bib coverall who was bald and thin, but shorter than Jon. Very much out of place in the garage setting and rolled up on its spindle was a blue wrestling mat.

Jon grasped a vertical, steel I-beam girder and inched up the wall using his hands to pull on the column post and his feet to push against the cinder block until he reached the ceiling 30' above. He then moved along the a steel rafter to the centerline of the building and then proceed along the long axis of the roof joists weaving first over then under supporting triangle trusses until he got to the far wall 50' away and reversed his technique to descend. He didn't wait, then broke to a brisk jog to a structure that looked like this:

Jon vaulted the fence, then proceeded to do more of the same—climbing the girders, shimmying down the vertical steam pipes, then moving to the adjacent twin assemblage, rinse, repeat. More running through the high elevation, semi-desert, mesquite laden pathways to another node called the Water Reactor

Research Test Facility where they Batmanned up a prepositioned rope to get to the top of a 30' tall white, rust streaked spherical natural gas storage tank and ran down the steel ladder that corkscrewed down to the concrete base pad. Jon sprinted back to the garage. Jason was all snot-bubbled up by the time he caught up with Jon who preemptively said, "Jack, all yours."

The same, slight grease monkey in bibs had changed into universal roughs' attire. Jack stepped briskly forward, stood tip-toed and peaked over Jason's much broader shoulders to see Kim maybe another 15 seconds inbound, and nearly whispered, "Son, if you ever leave a fucking man behind like that again, you are done here. We tracking?"

Jon had gotten into his Dodge pickup and headed to his barracks room. Forming these special teams was a process, and they were not under any hard stop timeline—i.e., the firm was going to do this right. They would go forward only when ready. Still, he wondered if he were doing enough, one, to prepare them, and two, was HE doing enough? Could HE do more? He was only a contractor here, and an independent contractor at that. As an IC, for example, he had no benefits, just a salary paycheck, and pretty much no authority beyond executing the POI he did help devise. He appreciated that this up and coming extraordinary generation of Patriots were at the pointy end of the spear as he had once been; they were galvanized by the events of 9/11 and craving to participate, to sacrifice if need be. Could he do more than just mentor, just train these great Americans? He had no one with whom to share his darker thoughts, and sometimes, when so encumbered, he spun down, down, down into a pit of guilt. A scrap of poetry by Henry Vaughn did little to buoy his gnawing and ravaging depredations.

There is in God, some say,
A deep but dazzling darkness, as men here
Say it is late and dusky, because they
See not all clear.
O for that night! Where I in Him
Might live invisible and dim!

Chapter 4

2002, Idaho National Laboratory

For the next 2 days, the pair went back and forth from the GSM network infrastructure back at SMC proper and out to Track 5, all within the clearly marked boundaries of the mammoth TAN complex. Their comfort with the baseline SIGINT equipment had progressed to the point that Arthur was waiting for them prior to another iteration of unimproved road evasive driving with Jack. Arthur showed them how to access the secret compartment to the modified TYPHON, how to bypass a kill switch that precluded inadvertent powering up at an inopportune time, and how to power down and stow the equipment back to its concealed recess.

After lunch on the second day, Jack let them know they would be doing some weapons training and they should follow his truck to the range.

At the range, which was merely a wadi right along which they walked in silence for maybe 500 meters from the road on which they had just been travelling, Jack walked to a steel shipping container, and keyed the padlock to open the door. He brought out a small foldable table, went back into the shipping container, and after rooting around with a flashlight in a walk-in vault further in the back, he brought out a Tupperware box.

Both Kim and Jason had shot handguns extensively, so the basics were dispensed. Jack handed out eyes and ears and said, "OK, folks. You are going to learn to draw and shoot under stress and learn when to carry operationally that is consistent with your cover, intended operational acts and anticipated threat. In most cases, you should not be carrying based on what I know of your mission.

If you do indeed have to carry and have something other than your dick to pull out, pardon my French, it'll be something very small, low caliber, but very concealable. We'll train with what you'll receive in country when the time is appropriate. We used to go with a Beretta 21 Bobcat, but found it jams way too much. Look, a .22 long rifle auto is bound to jam, but that one was out of control. Now we use this: a Seecamp LWS-32 with Winchester Silvertip hollow points. We'll probably go through several holsters until I pick the one that's the best fit for each of you."

With that, they took targets out of the shipping container, and with a critical eye for detail, Jack made slight corrections to their stance or how they sighted the tiny weapon, and they shot double action controlled pairs for the next several hours. Two shots, in the head, every time. Lock and clear, range breakdown, police up the brass, weapons cleaning. Dismissed and take your instructions from the white board.

On the ride home from the range, a white Land Rover with a graphic bearing the letters SPSC beneath a red oval and cedar tree superimposed over crossed arrows was parked menacingly next to the road leading into the Ville. The two bearded occupants' eye-fucked them as they drove past but did not pull out in pursuit. When they thought the day couldn't get too much worse, they walked into their apartment and saw the instructions on the white board: 'Report to Classroom 6, 31

SMC immediately. Bring the laptop.'

Since the SMC building was only a block away, they chose to walk. They walked with purpose, but still took the time to couple their hands and gaze into each other's eyes and smile. It was actually getting pretty easy to do, Jason thought. At the threshold of Room 6, they met Jon and were quite surprised. To allay their clearly evident trepidation, he said, "In this setting, it's all admin, and I want you to call me Serpico. That's my old call sign, but I'll refer to you only as Kim and Jason. Back on the streets, I'll revert to being Jon Prescott, but right now I want to introduce you to tomorrow's plan of the day."

The pair sat down and Serpico took his post at the white board/ movie screen. He started to lay out the block of instruction, "This is a task you'll need to be fully up to speed on when you go forward and you may have some familiarization with the concepts if you've already done pre-crisis activities overseas. What we'll focus on is conducting an airfield site survey. Again, on your laptop, you'll have the entire framework and checklist, so you won't have to take notes for stuff like this." He flipped up his first slide:

Plot Points of NAVAIDS

Electronic NAVAIDS	Plot Point (Horizontal)	Plot Point (Elevation)
Air Route Surveillance Radar	Axis of antenna rotation, if covered center of cover	Ground level through plumb line
Airport Surveillance Radar (ASR)	Axis of antenna rotation, if covered center of cover	Ground level through plumb line
Instrument Landing System (ILS)	(5)	(5)
Localizer (LOC)	Center of Antenna support structure	Ground level through plumb line
Middle Marker (MM)	Center of Antenna Array	Not required (6)
Inner Marker (IM)	Center of Antenna Array	Not required (6)
Back Course Marker (BCM)	Center of Antenna Array	Not required (6)
Outer Marker (OM)	Center of Antenna Array	Not required (6)
Glide Slope (GS)	Center of Antenna support structure	Ground level through plumb line (2)
Distance Measuring Equipment (DME) not frequency paired (ILS/DME)	(1)	(3)
Distance Measuring Equipment (DME) not frequency paired	Center of Antenna Cover	Center of Antenna Cover
Frequency paired with Localizer (LOC/DME)	(1)	(3)
Frequency paired with Non-Directional Beacon (NDB/DME)	(1)	(3)
Frequency paired with Microwave Landing System Azimuth Guidance (MLSAZ/DME)	(1)	(3)
Frequency paired with VHF Omni Directional Radio Range/Distance Measuring Equipment (VOR/DME)	(1) Center of Antenna Cover	(3) Ground level through plumb line
Fan Marker (FM)	Center of Antenna Array	Not required (6)
Localizer type Directional Aid (LDA)	Center of Antenna support structure	Ground level through plumb line
Microwave Landing System Azimuth Guidance (MLSAZ)	Phase center reference point	Phase center reference point
Microwave Landing System Elevation Guidance (MLSEL)	Phase center reference point	Phase center reference point
Non-Directional Radio Beacon (NDB)	Center of Antenna Array	Not required (6)
Simplified Directional Facility (SDF)	Center of Antenna support structure	Not required (6)
Tactical Air Navigation (TACAN)	Center of Antenna Cover	Ground level through plumb line
VHF Omni-Directional Radio Range (VOR)	Center of Antenna Cover	Ground level through plumb line
VHF Omni Directional Radio Range and TACAN (VORTAC)	Center of Antenna Cover	Ground level through plumb line
Differential GPS	Phase Center of Antenna	Phase Center of Antenna
Microwave Landing System (MLS)	Phase center reference point	Phase center reference point

He continued unperturbed by the look of shock on their faces, "I know it's a lot, but we are going to weave this in with the other evolutions over the next few days. You'll be able to determine what the general soil conditions are (e.g., rock, clay, sand); identify and locate obstructions adjacent to runways, taxiways, and parking aprons; how bulk fuel storage receives jet fuel (tank truck, tank car, pipeline, tanker/barge]). You may use a clinometer to determine runway or approach slopes; you'll get detailed instruction on how to use your modified Canon EOS Rebel T4i camera that, again, has a hidden partition SD card.

All this, done in a low-vis, clandestine manner. It is essential work if there are ever contingencies that arise for your area of operation. A finished product, and by that, I mean an obviously more crude, hand drawn sketch, might look something like this:"

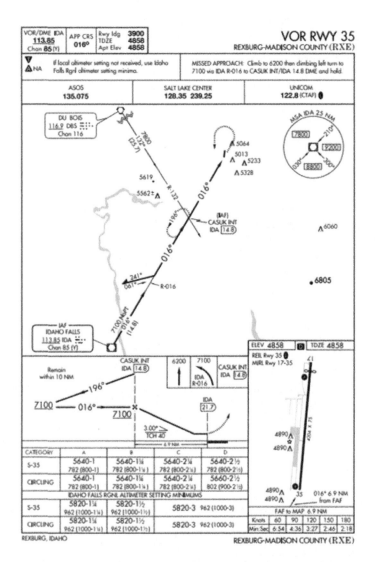

Serpico continued, "RJ will be your instructor for this. He will not only teach you not only the camera work, but he'll show you some electronic surveillance type equipment that will be able to determine the freqs and locate the Instrument Landing

System or the VHS Omni-Directional Radio Range shown on the previous slides.

As always, the equipment you use here is what you will use operationally. Belay that last statement. During travel times between training areas, always have your Sirius satellite radio on Channel 54 while you are driving. Sorry, the music is jazz, but we have a special relationship with Sirius and therefore we control that channel's transponder. The music is just cover for action. Your receiver has a modified chipset over which you can hear taskings or threat warnings that are encoded via a spread spectrum stream only you can receive. This is only a backup, one that certainly couldn't be used if you were driving guests around town. But I want you to at least monitor it when its safe. This particular item won't travel with you, and to be honest we are just using ya'll somewhat as guinea pigs to test it for use here in the US beam footprint, so this is the exception to the rule regarding operational equipment."

Jon paused for a moment. He added, "Jack will introduce you to the Rokon 2-wheel all-terrain vehicle. It's an off-road motorbike that has both wheels as drive wheels. It's a goat that can go anywhere and might be used in an E&E mode, for example. You'll use them or some Yamaha dirt bikes to get around in wadis on some long-range recons we have planned out in the desert. That's it for now."

Kim raised her hand. She actually raised her hand and said, "Serpico, we do have something to report. On the way back from Track 5, we saw a host nation Security Force patrol car and they were overtly mad dogging us but did not follow."

Serpico said, "Well, the game is afoot then, isn't it? You had better get cracking on writing a SPOT report to Jon hadn't you?"

Chapter 5

2002, Idaho National Laboratory

The next few weeks were a whirl of varying activity for the operative pair and those activities took many forms: classroom instruction on the 'special' laptop's myriad of internet enabled COVCOM capabilities; primers on how terrorists/criminal organizations conduct surveillance with counter measures practiced at Track 5; weapons manipulation such as draw stroke, loading/unloading and malfunction drills that was augmented with nasty combatives far beyond something like Krav Maga and focusing on strikes using gross motor skill muscle movements that are easily recalled under stress with the minimum intent to incapacitate, but more likely to kill; scaled iterations of crawl, walk and run permutations of airfield surveys; the invariable SDR through the Ville when meeting Jon at Track 5 for his latest torment – the road march (read: speed march); and finally, a few 'date nights' in nearby Rexburg which afforded a more robust road grid network to conduct proper SDRs prior to loading cache sites Jon that specified.

Clearly the 'date night' was mostly cover for action for the operational act of loading the cache site with Jason's sketches of the emerging and magical population explosion in the Ville boomtown. The SPSC patrols increased in lock step to both the pair's progress through the POI and in proportion to the town's expansion and infrastructure maturation. The pair had already been stopped at a midnight roadblock 'safety check' and were grilled by one Sergeant as what appeared to be an officer rooted through the 'special' laptops file structure with great concentration. There were no 4th Amendment Illegal Search and Seizure protections in Pineland.

One time they crossed the 'border' enroute to Rexburg and on the return through guard gate 676 (converted to a Pineland 'border entry inspection station') the pair were separated and individually processed through secondary. Stress levels were getting high as the workload piled up relentlessly. The last 'date night' was nearly a whole day of planning and executing the 'date', the drop and a PM with Jon at June's Place coffee shop on North 2nd East Street. The quality of the SDR between the operational act of the drop and meeting a CO had to be perfect. If surveillance was detected prior to the meet, they would have to abort.

Jon was seated when they rolled in. They had already completed a cover stop just prior, if nothing else, to clean up the sweat and appear fresh and unruffled. Looking quite academic in a tweed jacket with suede leather elbow patches and pipe, Jon greeted them like a professor meeting his favorite students, "Hello, you two. Kim, you get the espresso, two cubes, as you like it. Jason, the redeye. Right! Straight to it, shall we?"

They were in a corner booth, so they could speak fairly privately. After pleasantries were exchanged, complete with how's your Moms, Jon stated, "A lot of good work in your thesis, but we feel you're ready for a new phase in your studies. What we are going to do now is move you into an apartment in the Ville and you are going to learn some of the local culture and customs. Your guide through all this will be Janice, one of your prior teacher's assistants. She also will serve as interpreter—she has a great expanse of talents, yes? She will take you to the marketplace to shop; she will teach you how to cook at least a few middle eastern meals; she will guide you how to dress and fit in as best you can. You'll receive the address particulars on Channel 54 as you listen to a little mellow jazz on your drive back to campus."

And that was that for the business end of the meet; with a wink, Jon then asked the proprietor June if he could light up his pipe and proceeded to regale his favorite students with tales of his incredibly thorough research at BYU after which his postulates would withstand any counter argument regardless of rigor, and withstand them unscathed and with immeasurable panache.

After a week of Janice's patient but meticulous guidance on local culture, the pair received tasking via their pagers of all things. The brevity code was outwardly innocuous but had a clear mission: locate the mobile subscriber known to be in the Ville with the IMEI selector as provided. Here was an opportunity to use the Montero mounted TYPHON base station emulator in their operational backyard. Based on Janice's proffered menu and the façade of the Ville's developing movie set staging architecture, the pair suspected the Pineland scenario was malleable enough to accommodate the exact nuance of not merely any Middle Eastern city, but their exact follow on target location.

In whispered conversation in the bedroom at night, they shared the suspicion that they were not alone. The POI was clearly orchestrated to weave other couples into parallel but time-dispersed training events—all of this had not been built just for them. And just as clearly, each pair's plan of the day was designed to allow a round robin for all the participants, but no acknowledgement or interaction between them.

It was all compartmented, but they had seen several vehicles moving into places they had just vacated that clearly were not surveillance but occurred frequently enough to take notice over the expanse of time they had been there. That might also explain the different color Tupperware bins that Kim had noticed in the vault when Jack wasn't looking. Kim also noted the Montero was blue, her hijab was blue, the Tupperware bin was blue, their matching Mammut backpacks were blue. These observations did not appear on any of their reporting; they kept that little nugget to themselves.

When there were multiple taskings, they had to break off as singletons to get the work done, as this was the case. Muslim women don't drive around alone; in a lot of countries they just don't drive—so Jason pulled the intercept duty. Whereas this truly was one of Kim's strengths, he had to make it happen by himself. Kim spent the day at the bazaar acquiring new food stuffs for the pantry, this time without Janice.

When both returned to the apartment, Janice had a surprise. Clearly, the apartment had been selected for its proximity to a microwave tower just a few blocks away, but in all the excitement of moving in and learning a variety of soft skills, that detail hadn't registered. Janice was standing by a parabolic reflector antenna fitted with what looked like a 8 Ghz waveguide with a coaxial cable running through a splitter to an HP spectrum analyzer and to what looked like the heavy, carved mahogany coffee table in the living room.

Janice smiled and said, "Hi, Kim. Hi, Jason. Relax. We are going to go over some of the CDs that hide your mission equipment such as this analog/digital converter, BACKTRACK receiver, RAMORA demodulator, HALFLEX demultiplexer and follow on processors to service that antenna. You've already seen the equipment—this is all the same, just miniaturized and with the appropriate step up voltage converters for the Ville's power grid built into the coffee table."

She spent an hour showing them how to break down and assemble the adjoining triangle sections that together comprised the parabolic dish, the Pelco base with servo controller, the cabling and how to stow all that in a hidden compartment behind the bed headboard.

Janice explained, "OK. I do have a deviation from the norm, but it comes from Jon. He will confirm enroute on the sat radio, but you two are tasked to check in to the Wyndham Super 8 for the next few nights and conduct a full airfield survey of the Rexburg-Madison County Airport. Don't forget your passports, clock starts now." And with that, she turned on her heel and walked out of the apartment.

The reconnaissance took two days, both day and night, and since it was outside of Pineland, was considerably less stressful. They still had to be low-vis due to the real-world security guards and demonstrate just plain OPSEC discipline to get the job done right. Jason's sketches had improved, and Kim was a wizard at transforming them into a digitized format for storage on an SD card. As rendered on the 'special' laptop, one looked like this:

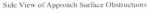

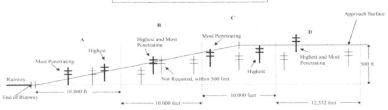

Obstruction representation in an approach area shall include the highest and most penetrating object/obstruction in the.

A - First 10,000 feet of the approach area
B – 10,000 - 20,000 feet of the approach area
C – 20,000 - 30,000 feet of the approach area
D – 30,000 - 42,332 feet of the approach area

The encrypted SD card was to be passed to an agent in a 'brush' pass on the BYU campus. This was followed by an SDR to meet Jon for a PM at the Madison Memorial Hospital cafeteria. Jon was already seated, as usual, but enthused, "All right, folks. This is it. This is your graduation. Here are your separate tickets for some R&R at your respective home domiciles. You'll reunite soon enough. No time for a lot of fanfare, but I'll say this. You both have done exceedingly well in the technical curriculum and, to me, I am very pleased in your coming together as a high-performance team and as a believable couple. I'll send an AAR to your gaining unit and to each or your supervisors. Be at ease, it'll be more than complimentary and to the point: you're ready.

I'll say one last thing. I want to thank you both for your service. Your deeds will likely far eclipse mine. I couldn't be prouder and more appreciative for what you are about do, and I thank God we still have American men and women like you. Keep your head on a swivel and God speed."

Chapter 6

1997-99, Ft. Meade and points east

For Jon Prescott, the late nineties were a busy time. He was a young Captain and subject to the illogical whims of his heart, just like any other young man. Still jet lagged, he was having Sunday brunch at the Dragon Hill hotel in Seoul when he saw her for the first time. Just like in the movies—their eyes met, there was immediate mutual interest, and it went from there. He was an American soldier, she a Canadian citizen on sabbatical teaching English to affluent Korean's children.

Shortly after she returned to Toronto, Jon continued his personal quest to serve in a special mission unit, so he attended a selection program, returned to the states, completed follow on specialized core competency training and awaited his initial operational assignment. He was disappointed when he learned he would PCS to Ft. Meade, MD and not to the undisclosed location where the Ops squadron was based.

As a good soldier, he followed his lawful orders and reported in as a liaison to the National Security Agency. His duties were twofold: perform liaison to a Joint Program Office and get branch qualified as a Major while assigned as a Troop operations officer. Jon did an SDR and drove to the SIGINT squadron HQ, the old Post brig off Huber Road. He changed out of his smooths in the locker room and reported in to the Commander in his Class-A uniform and Corcoran's as he always had, relaxed grooming standards be damned. This is the way it's done.

41

Jon knocked on the Commander's door, was called in, centered himself in front of the desk, came to attention, and hammered a snappy salute, "Sir, CPT Prescott reporting for duty as ordered!"

The man behind the desk was nonplussed to say the least. Whereas everyone else buzzing around the HQ was either in roughs, slicks, smooths or Nomex jumpsuits, the commander generally changed in to his BDUs, as he often had meetings with senior officers elsewhere throughout the day. The commander was one of few unit members not on the Department of the Army Special Roster (DASR) but he was indeed a duly charged O-5 commanding officer here at CISD and said, "Hello, Serpico. Welcome aboard. Not a lot of formalities here, throw in a Sir once and a while and I'm happy. I go by Guido, or Boss if you prefer. I see by the squashed bug on your lapel and the SF and Ranger tabs, you were already a little bit different as far as being an intelligence branched dude. Your troop commander and rater, Warthog, is over there to my left, your right, thus creating the mirror effect. He'll walk you through in processing and cover. Off you go."

And that is how it began, his life in the unit. After Jon changed back into his civvies, Warthog brought him to Security for read-ons and then to the team room. Warthog began, "Lots to go over. Much of your time will be spent getting or shaping taskings from JPO, coming back here and working with me and the Sergeant Major on mission analysis and plans, then creating CONOPS to support the JPO mission of intercepting foreign intelligence over fiber optic networks. This troop, A troop, exists purely to support the JPO. The other troops may do force protection or target development SIGINT while deployed in safe houses supporting the Tier-1 dudes, or as sensor operators on the various multi-mission aircraft.

Unless otherwise directed, we keep our distance from other operations. We have our hands full as it is, and I've needed an Opso for some time now. Still, I'm going to lose you for two weeks because you need a primer on a technology that is cutting edge and we need everyone up to speed so we can get in front of it. The short answer is: the Internet is just beginning and the hundred-pound heads in the Pentagon and the Fort believe it's going to grow in orders of magnitude, so transport is going to be a huge collection opportunity.

You will go in true name, under DOD cover as an officer assigned to the Defense Information Support Agency (the 'DISA') and you'll learn the basics of optical networking at a company in Hanover, MD called Ciena. Ciena incorporated in 1992 and just went through an initial public offering, or IPO, in February."

Warthog continued, "Their pioneering innovation is a technology called Dense Wavelength Division Multiplexing and basically that means breaking the light spectrum down into separate colors like red, green, blue to carry messages in each discrete frequency and maximizing the capacity of a single strand of glass fiber optic cable. We're talking Gigabits, not Megabits. Massive data flows.

For the next few days, check into a hotel in Falls Church and focus on area familiarization, particularly Leesburg Pike and the Seven Corners area so you can at least sound credible regarding DISA's AO. Come back, meet the team for a few days, then next week you'll join a class of civilian telecom engineers at Ciena. Cool?"

That week, Jon was so bamboozled he didn't say anything during the Ciena class. He completed the class, came back to the team room, gave a quick back brief where upon hearing his discomfort, an NCO recommended he take a basic networking course. Since they didn't have the budget to send him to Cisco in California, he went to Lucent Technologies in New Jersey using the same DISA cover. There he learned the vagaries of packet networks, internet protocols, switching, servers, routers and the other backbone elements comprising the Internet over 56kb twisted pair copper wiring prevalent to the time. It was still a leap ahead, but the concepts he learned in Hanover made more sense now.

For the most part, life was good. Work was fine, but his love life with Lisa, the woman he had met in Korea was complicated by the distance and time spent apart. She had her own career, hell, she had a Master's degree and was working on a second one and was not partial to marriage and living as an Army dependent here in the United States. He was more than committed to a way of life to which he had dedicated 10 years in pursuit. A clash of wills ensued no matter how great the emotions they both felt.

Jon spent less time in the team room than with the JPO planners at the Fort and sometimes in Langley. The JPO was a joint effort between the CLANSIG authorities of NSA and the HUMINT and covert action authorities of CIA. The first cross-

Atlantic fiberoptic cable called AC-1 was being laid to Bude, UK with a branch eventually going across the Channel to Germany. NSA had an arrangement with GCHQ to share a facility to tap into the cable. Jon was part of the pre-deployment site survey (PDSS) to the UK to determine requirements of how best to support that build out.

A consortium of telecom providers was funding this mammoth effort, one of which was Global Crossing, headquartered in New Jersey. Jon was unfortunately getting well acquainted with Interstate 95 traffic and New Jersey and its weird jug handles which were great for SDRs. In all the planning sessions, Jon got glimpses of the investments to make this project a reality:

Jon also kept up on current trends in telecom by reading trade publications like Lightwave with snippets of information such as, "Global Crossing recently announced plans to build the Mid-Atlantic Crossing, an undersea fiber-optic cable that will connect with AC-1. Service on AC-1, which spans more than 14,000 km and connects the United States, the United Kingdom, the Netherlands, and Germany, is scheduled to begin in May 1998. The system will be built in a self-healing ring configuration and use wavelength-division multiplexing (wdm) technology (see Lightwave, June 1997, page 7)." He knew all this, but he liked to be abreast of what information the public had access to if they were

45

inquisitive. It generally paid off in meetings with the commercial service providers as they had a language far different from military folk and you had to blend-in to the crowds at technical forums and trade shows.

A lot of fellows in the troop as well as the NSA engineer eggheads with whom he liaised followed this practice. It was necessary as the emergence of the internet was every bit as disruptive as when AT&T was split into seven smaller regional companies in 1984. All the planners involved in the operation to exploit AC-1 worked long hours to come up with a CONOP that would work and operate in utter secrecy. The concept they began to put their faith into was a practice just emerging to reduce failures in internet web pages. To balance the load between or among several servers being accessed by large audiences, internet service providers (ISPs) like MindSpring created a mirror site as a complete copy of a website or web page and placed it under a different URL that was identical in every other way.

The fiber optic equivalent was to duplicate the incoming signal at the beach manhole in a device called a Y-junction beam splitter waveguide coupler. This coupler sent identical data packets to both the 'original' cable landing site and a 'mirror' CLS. The splitter would need to be purpose built for both the range of spectrum and the enormity of capacity it would have to handle. CIA Directorate of Science and Technology (DS&T) let multiple sole-source contracts to cleared vendors in a race to get this critical component designed, fabricated, tested and ready to install. The concept looked something like:

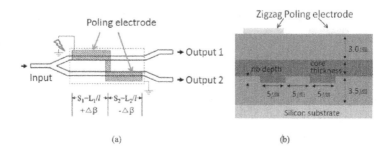

(a)   (b)

Both outputs 1 and 2 would terminate in identical submarine line terminating equipment (SLTE) and power feeding equipment (PFE) that comprise the corresponding CLS 1 and 2. Very imaginatively, the clandestine collection site at Bude, UK was called CCS_Bude with its twin at the beach landing site across the Channel in Sylt, Germany called CCS_Sylt. For the purpose of keeping this development under the radar, JPO had entire mockups fabricated at the Nevada Test Site where, in a terrestrial format, the teams could do a 'dry' run rehearsal.

On top of all this activity, a civil war in Europe had begun in July 1995 where an extermination of mostly Muslims occurred in Srebrenica, one of the small mountain towns protected by the U.N. in Eastern Bosnia. Although the Clinton administration had run away from keeping Somalia from sinking into a failed state in 1993 and nearly identically had buried its head in the sand when genocide reared its very ugly head in Rwanda in 1994, Bosnia was right smack dab in the middle of Europe where new atrocities were being committed. We have to do SOMETHING the liberals and do-gooders wheedled. So 'something' was done under the Dayton Peace Accords, and there was much rejoicing and Jon was gumbyfied and deployed to Bosnia.

The idea of Jon going overseas with its increasing physical

distance and inverse decreasing emotional commitment that comes with a deployment potentially into harm's way went over like a lead balloon with Lisa. She confided she had bought a duplex in Hamilton, a suburb of Toronto. This did not sound like a person in love and on the verge of marriage in the US. After more heated debate over the landline, Jon ended the relationship. He was torn between love, true love, and duty.

In Bosnia, Jon was still assigned to the unit but attached to MND (SW) in the British sector, ostensibly as the Yank/US LNO. Jon reported directly to the MND (N) G3 and gave him status if there were any cross-sector CT operations that might take place. Jon 's true mission as a singleton, under Operation AMBER STAR and reporting to Trooper at Buckeye base in Pale, was to provide technical support to the Brit SAS troop stationed at Banja Luka in the conduct of Persons Indicted for War Crimes (PIFWCs) captures. His dual reporting chain was to Sir Cedric Delves, the Brit MND(SW) commander and former SAS hero from the Falklands.

Technical support included the unit flying the Multi Mission Aircraft (MMA) King Airs out of Split, Croatia and conducting geolocation for SIGINT targets under Cooper Aerial high-altitude mineral exploration mapping cover that marketed image processing and plotting capabilities and with 'full rectification, translations, compression, calibration, and algorithms to provide the necessary product.' Tech support also include a new Agency play toy called a G-Nat, the Predator's predecessor. The G-Nat was purely a surveillance drone, there were no Hellfire missiles on a drone in those days. The PIFWC hunt was America's first foray into manhunting at scale.

The 6 months overseas went by without a hitch. In Jon 's mind, peacekeeping was crap: it was boring, a grievous misuse of combat power, it just wasn't war and he had little interest in it. A few days later after his return to CONUS, a group called Al Qaeda took credit for bombing US embassies in Dar es Salaam, Tanzania and Nairobi, Kenya. Unit members on alert status were paged to come in and start contingency planning and just as abruptly told to stand down and go home.

The United States of America's response was to let fly a handful of cruise missiles without any eyes on target into the mountainous wastes of Afghanistan to no effect. A man called Usama Bin Laden laughed at our facile response and released a fatwa for all Muslims to kill Americans. The US responded to that provocation with precisely nothing.

A few days later, Jon Prescott put in a DA 4187 to opt out of active duty.

Chapter 7

2003-2005, George Washington University

The work at INL was simultaneously gratifying and intellectually suppressive for Jon. He felt he could still mentor the next generation, but at the same time knew deep inside his particular skillset was becoming more and more obsolete as the GWOT took a massive upswing with the invasion of Iraq. While his skills stagnated and were rooted in the Cold War and the 20th century, new TTP emerged as MG Stan McCrystal transformed JSOC into a finely tuned machine. He had kind of liked the Falls Church area, so he moved there to attend grad school at GWU and work towards a master's degree in systems engineering. He was running out of time to use his GI-Bill, so now was the time to apply himself to new studies.

To bring in some cash while he went to school, Jon became active in the Reserves and worked part time in the operations directorate at J3-SOD, the special operations (SO) proponent of the Joint Staff. He was assigned as an action officer in the Operational Support Branch (OSB) and handled staff packages related to the SAP and joint CIA/DOD special activities. The way he summarily quit he likely would never be assigned to the unit ever again, but he did have the pedigree and was useful in that regard. JS staff packages greatly are comprised of DEPORDs and EXORDs—authorizations, even at small team or singleton level, to deploy and conduct missions OCONUS, sometimes requiring SECDEF or POTUS approval, depending on sensitivity and risk. It was not sexy work.

However, with the fallout from 9/11, the work became more urgent because there was no SO advocate at the J5 where higher level Plans are normally staffed. At J3-SOD, he, CDR Dan Brown, LTC Tom Moose, and SGM Frank Denham wrote the campaign plans for the Global War on Terror (GWOT) that 1) enumerated the general framework of terrorist pursuit codified in the statement 'capture or kill, C/K', 2) defined the levels of incursion as OPE, AFO, D/CT, and 3) tasked USSOCOM as the DOD proponent for the actual global campaign which eventually became the 7500 series of CONPLANs. The original document approved by SECDEF was called the AQSL EXORD, the Al Qaeda Senior Leadership execute order, in which there were 7 top tier AQ leaders targeted for C/K.

As Iraq spooled up into a frenzy to counter the unanticipated insurgency often bank rolled by Iran, it became apparent the AQSL thing was too restrictive in scope; the concept was revised to create the AQN EXORD. AQN meant AQ Network, and it opened up whole vistas beyond UBL, Zawahiri (AZ), Kahlid Sheik Mohammed (KSM) and the others regarded as the core senior leaders. Most of all these planning/tasking documents fell under SPECAT (Special Category) for Focal Point classification designations.

Recall the mission sets of the AQSL EXORD: OPE, AFO and D/CT. Operational Preparation of the Environment (OPE) was setting in line a clandestine infrastructure in the host nation so the US could perform unilateral actions if necessary as well as bilat relationships with the HN. That meant, setting up SHs through surrogates, doing LZ/HLZ/BLS surveys, setting up navigational beacons to vector in aircraft flying NOE, procuring local vehicles, recruiting an indig network to do some of this stuff, that sort of thing. Advanced Force Operations (AFO) was more active target development, and in a blink of an eye could flip to Decisive/Counter Terrorism (D/CT) as a deliberate or spur of the moment action of an objective, either C/K. Each layer required approval, sometimes SECDEF, sometimes POTUS depending on sensitivity. For example, a hit in Israel would definitely require POTUS approval. All this was defined in a matrix by country in the various EXORDS.

He did what he felt was junior high school level military duty as a Reservist, but he partnered with a Navy lieutenant commander working at the Office of Naval Research (ONR) on a thesis paper on Underwater Unmanned Vehicles (UUVs) for their Capstone project at GWU. The most interesting part of the research was going to the Naval Surface Warfare Center at Carderock, MD. ONR was conducting tests on some UUV prototypes for CLUSTER POSEIDON in the indoor rectangular deep water basin that is 6.7 m (22 ft) deep, 575 m (1886 ft) long and 15.5 m (50.96 ft) wide at Carderock; they used some of the unclassified data that was compiled in the acoustic signature measurement tests to inform their thesis conclusions.

All this was fine and good, but Jon was literally tormented when alone at night by thoughts that he was derelict in seriously contributing during a time of war.

Salvation appeared in the form of an 8" x 11" brown envelope laying on his floor under the front door mail slot. It was an envelope bearing a return address specifying the Department

54 of the Army. There was a clear plastic window in which he could make out his address and music to his ears:

"Pursuant to Executive Order 13239 signed on September 14, 2001, you are relieved from your present reserve component and ordered to active duty in support of Operation Iraqi Freedom…"

Chapter 8
2005-2007, Balad Air Base, IQ

While Jon was undergoing his initial mobilization in processing at the CRC at Ft. Benning, Jamal Madan al-Tamimi, aka JMT or Objective Dawa, had returned from being on the lam in Bahrain where he had learned the EFP trade under the nom-de-guerre Faleh Abu al-Shaabi. JMT was establishing an initial support network of Iraqi Shia adherents in Najaf, nearly 180 kilometers south of Baghdad. This location was not a strategic, significant targeting opportunity, but merely a safe haven waypoint amongst a population of brothers in which he could disappear.

His immediate concern was invisible absorption into the ummah; to arrange eventual access points to road networks astride Highway 1 and Highway 2; to reposition brothers to Kirkuk that had been embroiled in the struggle to liberate Fallujah; and to establish a cadre of trusted couriers to inform his operations in Sadr City, Kirkuk, and Tikrit. It was clear the Americans were here to stay at least for now; his was a dance of death over a longer expanse of time than he wagered they were willing to invest. He had both the resolve and funding to expend his resources wisely and with great patience.

Jon's orders assigned him as an intel analyst at CENTCOM HQ in Tampa. Fuck that. That just wouldn't do. Upon arrival, he immediately evangelized with some of his SF brethren right next door at SOCOM in the J3X and offered his services in any kind of liaison capacity and he let the full bird in charge there devise a way to broach the idea to his counterpart at CENTCOM. The deal was this: he would remain assigned to the CENTCOM J2X shop, be attached to the JSOC J2X shop, and because of his civilian training as a systems engineer and project manager, Jon would assist in the expansion of a new capability in the military overhead surveillance arsenal: the drone. Jon would fully inform CENTCOM of infrastructure development in both Iraq, Afghanistan, and Yemen.

This was as it was meant to be, Jon thought. In a bizarre twist, when he had stood in his first formation at the CRC in Ft. Benning, he noted another officer prior to falling in. This Major looked like Vinny bag-o-donuts the shitbag, recalcitrant malingerer based on the unshaven, disheveled ragbag, out-of-regs hair and crumpled uniform. He reeked of last night's send off to war or bachelor party booze that was seeping out of his pores. To his great consternation, this Major was the only one else in the formation wearing a flat green hat, a rifle green beret. Such was his unimpressive introduction to Rob, his eventual Hyde Park Place roommate. Rob was an SF branch reservist assigned to SOCOM who was on his second gig here in Tampa and he made the appropriate introductions to the J3X folks.

Jon and Rob would hang out after work at the various locales on Horatio or Swann. However, as pleasant as Tampa was in December (he and Rob went skydiving in shorts and a t-shirt at Zephyr Hills on weekends), Jon wanted to get in country and go to work. Soon enough, he got his wish and flew to Camp Doha, Qatar where he bunked in the barracks marked for TF-121, then moved along via Bagdad to his destination at Balad Air Base. There he was read-on to various programs, but his focus was POND STONE, the effort to greatly raise the number of orbit coverage available to support an increasingly urgent optemp of hits against HVTs.

Although he had been aware of the general flow of CT operations due to his time at J3-SOD, Jon learned his drone portfolio would expand to include basing in Djibouti and laying the clandestine ground work for a CIA base in Arba Minsch, Ethiopia. This was interesting all by itself—the SECDEF Donald Rumsfeld had been ruffling some feathers in the Pentagon and inside the Beltway. From the Agency's point of view, DOD was encroaching on CIA equities in their aggressive pursuit of the GWOT. That was Rumsfeld. JSOC had a slightly different viewpoint and were willing to enhance operations by cooperating subserviently within an overseas CIA Chief of Station's AO, even in war zones clearly covered by the AUMF. The marriage of JSOC and CIA capabilities has been around since Vietnam at the very least, and McCrystal's expedient remedy was if it ain't broke, don't fix it.

Right here at Balad, he billeted at the airfield where the Air Force's 46th Expeditionary Reconnaissance Squadron was based. They flew the MQ-1B Predator UAV, the drone that had been developed to replace and enhance capabilities by its CIA predecessor, the G-Nat. Either variant was made by the same company, General Atomics. Jon 's job had little to do with payloads and the airframe's performance; his job was building out or maintaining the supporting airfield runway, generator power, hangar capacity, parking apron layout, billeting, ground control stations (GCS), aids to navigation, fork lifts and flatbeds, and the communications architecture required to tie the Preds back to the drivers and sensor operators. EO and IR video data was passed via LOS or UHF/Ku-Band satellite data link to the GCS. SAR framed imagery required a Ku-Band satellite link. This comm architecture was critical, as the aircraft were often flown by pilots at Indian Springs, in Nevada. The general comm layout looked like this:

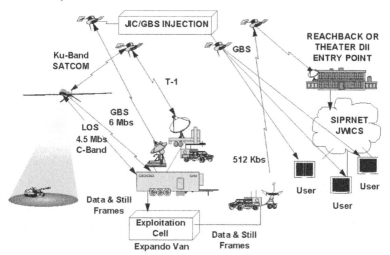

The Air Force airfields in Iraq and Afghanistan were a little easier due to their overt posture. Camp Lemonnier in DJ was a little odd as it fell in AFRICOM's footprint but had operations that bled over into CENTCOM's area of operations. On top of that, it was forced to share a single runway with Djibouti's only international airport, as well as an adjoining French military base. Jon was part of the source selection planning that awarded a $62 million contract to build an airport taxiway extension and an ammunition storage site to handle increased drone traffic at Lemonnier and support kinetic operations, respectively.

Pakistan hosted an Air Force activity in Shamzi, PK that was far more sensitive. The base in Shamzi, PK was not fully covert, but it was a lightning rod of political sensitivity for the President of Pakistan, General Pervez Musharraf. Although this base hosted the Preds that brought justice via Hellfire to many Taliban using Pakistan as a lily pad from which to launch attacks against NATO forces in neighboring Afghanistan, it wasn't really much of a secret to the local Baluch's despite Jon's efforts through cut outs and various tradecraft mechanisms. Anyone could go into a rug shop in Islamabad and buy a root dyed woven tribal prayer rug declaring "War Against Terror" along the top fringe. Featured amongst images of M-16s, AK-47s, and CH-47s, a design of a Predator labelled "Spy Plane" was affixed.

Most drone flights over the budding fester of strife and poverty called Yemen flew out of DJ, but the CIA was setting a path with the Kingdom of Saudi Arabia to create a base of operations in the southwestern desert of Saudi Arabia called Umm al Mehl Base. Flight times and fuel costs would be cut by 2/3rds and time on target increased by twice as long the loiter time gained by this new geometry. The base to be constructed would lie in the vast Rub' al Khali desert about 43 kilometers from the Yemeni border and be subcontracted to an Agency surrogate, the Abdullah A. M. Al-Khodari Sons Company. In this case, Jon only had to liaise with CIA on behalf of JSOC and keep apprised of progress. JSOC had similar equities and methods in the base at Arba Minsch. CENTCOM had no skin in that game, so Jon kept that to himself.

After six months in country, Jon only then could grasp the enormity of this undertaking. It was clearly far too much for him to accomplish over a one-year mobilization tour, so he requested, and was granted, a 6-month extension. A by-name request by JSOC to CENTCOM had ways of clearing any administrative obstacles. Even still, due to time zones, the pure complexity of the task, the variety of bureaucracies (and bureaucrats) such as NASA, NRO, NOAA as well as competing regional command's headbutting and the Agency's proclivity to steer payment to DOD, Jon found himself logging 16 hour days. He hammered away, travelled to his sites when able to or because of design decisions or patching labor disruptions, and finally he had a coherent, comprehensive, and executable schedule. He had CONOPs for both Yemen and Arba Minsch; multiple sites in Iraq and Afghanistan at or nearing initial operating capability (IOC) or full operating capability (FOC); Pakistan and DJ were both at FOC by the end of his tour.

His was good, solid management of a regional endeavor that was essential to saving American lives. Jon took great pride in joining a high-performance team that just plain made things happen during an extraordinary time. Even still, he declined the Bronze Star without a 'V' device for which he had been recommended; he felt a Bronze Star should be reserved not for meritorious service but only for valorous distinction and he had done nothing worthy of that recognition. He had been here long enough to know who the true heroes were; he saw these men every day, operators who sometimes went on multiple hits a night, men so focused on mission and keeping each other alive that those who did not walk in their shoes could not comprehend the sustained terror and emotional whiplash of their sacrifices. Ribbons were no consolation for the times they had to endure saying farewell to a fallen comrade with an inverted rifle, helmet, dog tags and combat boots framed by a mournful, brassy rendition of the 24 notes of 'Taps'.

By now, Jamal Madan al-Tamimi had consolidated his power in Ramadi. Here he laid his traps and devised his schemes with one intent in mind: Kill the infidel.

Chapter 9

2006- 2007, Tonopah Test Range (TTR), Nevada

Scrambling to find a job after his stint back on active duty, Jon could find nothing interesting in the DC area, so he rented his house in Falls Church out to a military couple both posted at the Pentagon. Poor saps, he thought. He ended up going back to being an independent contractor out west, this time in Nevada. He bought an Airstream travel trailer which would be challenging in the winters but was homey enough for his Spartan tastes. After over a year in a plywood B-hut, the Airstream was palatial.

At this point in the GWOT, a few things were very apparent to the senior leaders of its participants, particularly those who represented clandestine organizations, whether it was the firm, JSOC and its tier-1 units, or CIA. Although all these elements focused a great deal of energy toward developing actionable intelligence, each spent nearly the same amount of resources doing direct action on fully developed targets. The boots on the ground players were at extremely high risk. There had been mistakes, there had been some cluster fucks, and there were training deficiencies that needed to be rectified.

The POI at the Nevada Test Site focused on fixing one glaring deficiency: the recovery of isolated personnel who were under deep cover in hostile territory. DOD ran a scenario up in Fairchild Air Force base in Washington state that scratched the surface but was not fully suited to the rigors that covered personnel could face. In a broad brush, the scenario entailed 4 man teams conducting combat training in TTR, traveling to village south where they were compromised, the team then would escape and evade via a ratline to what was now called Creech Air Force base. There were surprises along the way and each team had to think on their feet.

The four person teams were often comprised of a mix of operator and support personnel, the common ground being operational placement in fully hostile territory. Only one class was run at a time and it began at TTR. For some, the initial training was a refresher course on SERE, but each team also conducted target reconnaissance, weapons qualification and a primer on target acquisition and the use of laser designators to mark those targets for smart bombs. The terminal guidance operations were often done in conjunction with Predator oversight from which certified JTACs had optics and eyes on to perform the weapons release on the terminal attack control.

The 4-PAX could relax and enjoy themselves at TTR. This was the fun part. Each day they would do PT, eat in the mess hall, go to the classrooms for instruction, maybe go to the range and fire either M-16s or familiarization training with AK-74s. They conducted their TGOs and target recons and occasionally did 5-mile runs. After all, they were still in friendly territory.

The real application of their training began across the 'border' in, to some, a familiar sounding country imaginatively called West Pineland whose security apparatus was the malevolently omnipresent SPSC. The 4-PAX were driven across the border and delivered to the outskirts of the town of Goldfield where they individually made their way to the Santa Fe motel with further instruction to proceed for a PM at The Little Church in Goldfield. Often, Jon could see at least one candidate wearing the issued black day pack as they motored along 4th street right past his Airstream's wrap around windows at Goldfield RV Park.

The 4-PAX team is then betrayed and rolled up by the SPSC at the meet site or depending on the composition of the 4-PAX team, sometimes rolled up in the secondary at the border crossing. In either case, fortunately after just a few hours of rubber hose, the team is heroically sprung from captivity by the insurgents battling the oppressive West Pineland regime and vectored along to points south via various recovery mechanisms along the ratline.

At times, the 4-PAX have to E&E by foot, at other times they are stuck under a tarp in a flatbed and whisked along Veterans Memorial Highway to small sites with some mock-up enhancements to bed down at an insurgent safe house. The 4-PAX make their way south to Mercury, where they are separated and 'repatriated'. There is a catch. Evaders comprising the 4-PAX team that are either technical operations officers, case officers or Tier-1 level operators then fly out of Desert Rock Airport to Las Vegas where as singletons they continue an urban scenario, but conduct operational tasks in 'payment' to their insurgent benefactors.

The reassembled graduates are then cycled through a follow-on course at Creech on how to develop an organized escape network in hostile territory. The participants followed a scenario encapsulated within the Pineland scenario that centered on the insurgents having the sympathetic ear of the loosely represented Alawite sect interspersed throughout the dominantly Sunni Pineland landscape. The Alawite role players render assistance much like Croatian priests did in WW II. Each individual then recruits an ally to construct a specific recovery mechanism in the villages astride Highway 95 on the North-South ratline to freedom from Goldfield to Mercury.

As an advisor on the Personnel Recovery Coordination Cell (PRCC) staff, Serpico acted as an exercise director of EMERALD NOMAD and was charged with coordinating all the logistics, role players and cadre required to create and operate the training lane, all the way from infil and combat skill applications at TTR, the initial isolation at Goldmine and the mechanisms to enable the escape to Mercury fell under his guidance and purview. The bolt-on scenario in Las Vegas was a compartmented element in which he was only a role player. Because his contract had no conflicts of interest with providing liaison support to the Predators flown by the 11th Reconnaissance Squadron at Creech, Serpico was authorized to maintain his Army Reserve participation for points as in individual mobilization augmentee (IMA).

The end state of this POI was to certify a recovery team that could conduct Non-conventional Assisted Recovery (NAR) operations for covered personnel escaping West Pineland. The recovery team was comprised of the 4-PAX that had just completed the transit. The 4-PAX received 4 days of classroom instruction and then were dispatched, one PAX per site. At each site stands a village populated by role players, resistance or insurgent auxiliary amongst that population, and an Alawite shrine. As a recovery team member, a singleton from the 4-PAX team would be inserted into a village and over the course of 5 days, and after figuring out who was who, build rapport (usually through some kind of manual labor) with the friendlies and perform assigned tasks.

Throughout the evolutions, the SPSC is aggressively searching for the evaders as well as anyone who might assist them.

At Site 1, aka Goldfield, the recovery team member sets the stage. He carries out this task as a case officer, one who has to build a longstanding relationship with the insurgents and understands he must earn his host's trust. He is introduced to Zack, the fellow for whom he will toil clearing brush and carrying rocks while conducting habitat and trail maintenance cleanup duty. Zack is a driver at Zero1 Ranch and Off-road Compound where Zero1 'provides clients with access to Nevada's unique past, diverse terrain and spacious beauty, either on two wheels or on four.' Once rapport is established, his task is similar to reception, staging, onward movement, and integration (RSOI) of the evaders being taken under the protective wing of the auxiliary of the insurgent force. The case officer provides the incoming evaders with a blood chit that requests the bearer be rendered every assistance (and offers a reward); provides a pointee-talkee to transcend language barriers; provides a SARNEG code, essentially a one-time pad (OTP) with a 10 letter word each letter corresponding to number 0-9; and lastly the next 48 hour's challenge and password. Finally, the case officer arranges transport at the Zero1 Ranch and Off-road Compound where Zack will whisk them along in 185-hp off-road Polaris RZR dune buggies to within a discrete distance to Site 2.

At Site 2, the recovery team member is introduced to an auxiliary agent that is a resident on the Timbisha Shoshone

65

Indian Reservation. To build rapport, the recovery team member learns how mesquite trees were always a focal point of Timbisha culture and spends many hours clearing away dead branches from each tree so harvesters can gather fallen mesquite pods. Once rapport is established, he procures a safe house and prepares a dead drop in which he relays signaling authentication procedures for the IR-25 Phoenix command entered recognition encoder, specifies a duress code word in case of compromise by the SPSC, and provides instructions for locating and servicing a cache site.

At Site 3, aka Beatty, NV, the recovery team member is introduced to an auxiliary agent that owns Beatty Mini-Storage. To build rapport, the recovery team member cleans out abandoned storage units and loads the content within to a flatbed trailer for transport down to Indian Springs. Once rapport is established, the auxiliary agent also reveals his name is Afwad and that he is a member of the Alawite sect and the recovery team member offers to go get a beer at the VFW on 3rd street with the intent of developing the agent for more significant support activities. Afwad offers an empty storage unit which the recovery team member uses as a cache site as well as a ride on the flatbed for the incoming evaders.

This cache site contains the following: a PRQ-7 survival radio, the IR-25 Phoenix strobe beacon, PVS-7-night vision goggles (NVGs) and extra batteries, VS-17 panel, MREs and a Suunto A-10 compass. To be centrally located at this point of the exercise, Serpico had already stationed his Airstream with Iridium sat phone at Space Station RV Park in downtown Beatty.

At Site 4, aka Mercury, NV, the recovery team member is

introduced to an auxiliary agent named Earl at the United States Postal Service facility on Buster Street. To build rapport, the recovery team member washes the USPS delivery truck, changes the tires, and helps load the day's mail sacks into the bins for sorting. Once rapport is established, Earl offers his services as an interpreter. The recovery team member takes Earl with him to accomplish a task: procuring a warehouse

to accommodate at least three 5-ton trucks for future contingencies. Earl is tasked to lay down VS-17 panels in the shape of a L with the long axis pointing east to mark an LZ in the middle of the one-mile jogging track oval next to the USPS facility once he hears helicopters inbound at roughly 9pm.

The recovery team member takes his place at the predetermined rally point by the electric substation north of town where he will conduct RSOI of the evaders and provide them the authentication codes to board the incoming bird. Once they link up, the evaders are to don the NVGs with IR turned on and follow the 'sparkle' of a laser marker that paints a 'yellow brick road' as seen through the goggles blazing the route from which they are not to deviate. Once on the bird, each evader will answer questions from his ISOPREP data.

Each recovery team member is then cycled to another site until he or she completes all the tasks at each site. This exercise was conducted for 6 classes a year. Over the course of nearly two years, Serpico met a lot or people across the entire clandestine community. One day, Serpico was approached by an individual who asked him to meet him on Friday night at the Oasis Bar in Indian Springs. "I just might have a job in mind if you're interested", the man said.

Chapter 10

2010, Ft. Meade, MD

While attending the Joint Forces Staff College, a bright, young student named Lt. Col. Eugene V. Becker wrote a master's thesis titled, <u>Mining and Exploitation of Rare Earth Elements in Africa as an Engagement Strategy in US Africa Command</u>. In his opening abstract, he quite bluntly stated some uncomfortable facts, "Rare earth elements (REE) are a key ingredient in high-technology products that are critical to defense, energy and other industries that impact national security and economic viability. The United States enjoyed a monopoly in rare earth mining and exploitation until the late 1990s when China gained monopoly status. They now supply over 95% of rare earths to the world. China's explosive economic growth has put them on a path to consume 100% of all the rare earths they produce in just a few years, leaving nothing for export."

In the online trade rag called Seeking Alpha, Robert Castellano's numbers didn't fully match up, but still pointed to rough waters for the US in regard to REE. His research nearly corroborated, "In our report "Rare Earths Elements In High-Tech Industries: Market Analysis And Forecasts Amid China's Trade Embargo," we estimate that the Chinese held 90.0% of capacity of rare earth oxides with 103,300 tons, but its share will drop to 67.2% in 2014 based on output of new mines coming onstream. China's capacity will only increase 10.4% to 114,000 tons between 2010 and 2014, whereas non-Chinese capacity will increase nearly 5-fold, from 11,500 to 55,800 tons."

REE was only one facet of economic pursuit churning in the maw of Chinese ambition that sought more influence and power and would hardly be contained by its own borders. For its own part, the United States was barely keeping its head above water and trying to recover from the Lehman shock of 2008. Still, if there were opportunity to be found in the REE market, the US under Obama was not taking full advantage.

An Institute for Energy Research commentary ripped, "The United States currently does not mine rare earth minerals but has large deposits of rare earth elements. Environmental regulations closed down the last rare earth mine in the United States at Mountain Pass in California. In 1966, the Mountain Pass mine had become the world's largest producer of rare earth elements. From the mid-1960s through the mid-1980s, the United States was the largest source of rare earth elements and was self-sufficient in their production.

By the mid-1980s, environmental and regulatory issues at Mountain Pass led to its near shutdown and eventually its demise as a working mine while the Chinese ramped up production… It seems like our President does not mind losing jobs and industry to the Chinese, whose economy has grown to the point of being the largest consumer of energy in the world… We can do more here to create jobs and provide secure energy if only the Administration would step aside from creating impediments."

Jon Bennett was a creature of habit. Out of professional development and self-interest, he continued with his practice of reading trade magazines, although they were mostly online now. Jon had worked long hours during his mobilization tour with then Major Becker in Balad. They remained friendly and kept in touch. Eugene, aka call sign 'Torch', sent a copy of his thesis which Jon read ravenously. True to Torch's style of conciseness, the manuscript had a single table which caught Jon's eye:

Defense Uses of Rare Earth Elements	
Lanthanum	night-vision goggles
Neodymium	laser range-finders, guidance systems, communications
Europium	fluorescents and phosphors in lamps and monitors
Erbium	amplifiers in fiber-optic data transmission
Samarium	permanent magnets that are stable at high temperatures
Samarium	precision-guided weapons
Samarium	"white noise" production in stealth technology

There you go, Jon thought, pretty much anything I have ever done is involved in this REE mess. Some other news caught his eye. He found an article on the TechZim website quite interesting:

Posted Thu 15 Jul 2010 by L.S.M Kabweza (@lskmakani)

The EASSy undersea fibre cable will go live tomorrow, 16 July 2010. The EASSy commercial launch follows the completion of three successful tests that have been carried out on the cable in the last few months.

EASSy (short for Eastern Africa Submarine Cable System) becomes the third undersea cable to land on the East African shores in just 2 year following the launch of SEACOM and TEAMs cables last year. With a capacity of 1.4 Terabits per second(Tbps), EASSy is the highest capacity cable to connect to Africa so far. SEACOM and TEAMs have a capacity of 1.2 Tbps each.

The EASSy cable has 9 landing points in Africa, stretching from South Africa through Mozambique, Madagascar, The Comoros, Tanzania, Kenya, Somalia, Djibouti up to Sudan. It is expected to be extended inland to 12 landlocked countries including Zimbabwe, Zambia, Botswana and Malawi. See picture above.

source: http://www.wiocc.net/map.htm

Of course, Jon was interested in anything telecom, and since his experience on the JPO and AC-1, he tracked fiber optic networks growth with great zeal. He grasped the connection between rare earth metals and how it would likely affect the availability and cost of the erbium that was used in the "amplifiers in fiber-optic data transmission" noted in Eugene's table. In his current job, also telecom related, Jon would travel to Africa and other cities in the world as a technical systems integrator on a combined Agilent Technologies and Tektronix team that provided product and services to the Data Acquisition (S3) directorate of NSA.

The Agilent portfolio centered around the Agilent E3238S Blackbird suite that included wireless intercept capabilities to reliably detect and decode MIL-STD-188-141 HF-ALE communications and had an additional VHF/UHF voice activity detection system that provided an integrated suite of automated tools to reliably detect and demodulate multiple voice signals in the band of interest. This system (35688E-VA2) used a technology that dramatically reduced false positive identifications common with other systems that only use single-pass frequency-domain techniques. It could also be integrated tightly with popular common direction-finding solutions to create a complete detection and geolocation solution.

Agilent equipment was used to Fix and Finish targets using push-to-talk radio communications, but not cell phones. Over the course of the last decade, high frequency (HF) Radio technology gained a significant advantage with the introduction of HF Automatic Link Establishment (HF ALE). This new standard was developed to automatically select an HF frequency that would support a communications link between stations in a network or point-to-point without operator assistance. This was useful for terrorists like Usama Bin Laden who quickly adopted this standard and currently use HF ALE radios for long-haul communications.

HF radio wave propagation can, if skipped off the stratosphere, go halfway around the world, not including the North and South poles. The Agilent HF ALE equipment was operated out of Guam (Site G) and Brandy station (Site B) near the Warrenton Training Center in Fauquier County, Virginia.

Tektronix developed, provided, deployed, and maintained modified protocol analyzers that normally were used to monitor the performance over hard-wired Ethernet connected core services within a GSM cellular network. The platform was called a K-15 and had originally been manufactured as a K-1297 Protokolanalyzer by Siemens Corp in Berlin, Germany. The modified K-15 was installed in the Mobile Switching Center (MSC) on the A-interface of a given network to conduct intercept, i.e, electronic surveillance, or SIGINT, and was considered to be outside of the normal portfolio, i.e, "beyond traditional accesses".

Tektronix did megadata collection for asset validation and HVT targeting overseas and supported sites in Montenegro (Site M), Kathmandu (K), Phenom Pehn (P), Data Lens (DL -- encompassing sites in Mombasa, Manda Bay and Nairobi, Kenya) and Cairo, Egypt (C).

The general idea of using a commercial piece of gear to conduct SIGINT was for plausible deniability purposes. It was gear that could be shared with a host nation on a bilateral op and not compromise NSA cryptography or methods. The entire program was called **'Echo'** and was derived from the 'E' in the Agilent E3238S product designation. It included 'beyond traditional accesses' relative to covert airgap collectors based off of embassy rooftops, and it was funded by the Special Collection Service (SCS). Its mission was essentially running SIGINT collectors on top of whatever they could reach line of site-wise from a US Embassy or US Dept of State Annex OCONUS.

Jon's job was merely keeping all the systems up to date with software patches, feature updates, application upgrades that increased capability and the logistics of moving personnel and equipment around a myriad of cover for action schema. It was great software engineering and development work interspersed with a smidge of tradecraft. However, much to his distaste, he was always under pressure from each commercial company to sell more, sell more, sell more. They were in it for the money—that's what they did-- make and sell a product for profit.

Nothing at all wrong with that, but Jon yearned for more operationally oriented work. Other companies like Raytheon and General Dynamics supplied the application engineers that went overseas and ran the intercept operations, and he occasionally traveled for design reviews or logistical coordination, but it just wasn't scratching the itch. Over the two years of this project, he had poked around and found a different avenue that killed two or three birds with one stone.

Chapter 11
2012, Herat, Afghanistan

Jon Bennett had been wrestling with his dreams and random thoughts for some time now. He was quite aware he was depressed. Not crazy, depressed. He had spent nearly 28 years on and off in the military, both officer and enlisted, in both the active duty and in the Reserves. During that time, he had deployed, yes, but for the most part felt unfulfilled. He still felt guilty he had not given his all. He also knew he had to get a grip—his work as a contractor was significant in that it still provided value to the war fighter. Yet, he could not shake his guilt that he was not in the warzone, fighting it out against the America's enemies.

That in itself was a concern. It seemed our foreign policy choices and strategies just didn't have the impact one might think should. Bosnia? Really? Iraq? Where we lost thousands of young American lives only to abandon that effort? If we were going to invade someone, why not Iran who took 52 Americans hostage for 444 days? We still owed those mother fuckers. Jon had spent two years on the NSA campus and had felt the unspoken sting as a second-class citizen slimy, money grubbing contractor, but he had also mastered many of the bureaucracies on that campus. To slake his guilt of insufficient duty, he volunteered to be mobilized through the Reserve Affairs office, with one condition: send me to a warzone.

He was to be a collection engineer for the rooftop covert SIGINT activities, specifically initially forward deployed to

Afghanistan. He would be a DoD guy authorized to participate in Title 50 covert action; the process was called being 'sheep dipped', i.e., loaned to CIA under the procedure of D triple S (DSSS -Defense Sensitive Support System) orders signed by the Army DCS, G-2 LTG Mary Legere and the SECDEF.

SCS is a joint CIA/NSA activity that conducts mid-point SIGINT out of US flagged activities like an embassy, consulate, or State Department Annex (even a warehouse). SIGINT tasking may be in direct support of HUMINT operations out of Station, like in the case of asset validation, or in direct support of tasking from the Ambassador (rare). SCS is also unique in that not only do you collect, but on site there are dedicated analysts and linguists on live collection missions for immediate break down (not sending it back to Ft Meade and waiting).

Unless for extended reach applications through SCS, intercept is limited to radio that is line of site from a given compound to include WiFi, HF ALE, PTT, cellular phone, and PCM links like microwave towers. There may also be special antennas with the appropriate modems and modulation processing for satellite down links where the facility is in the beam footprint. Cover is straight State Department diplomatic (dip) cover as a member of the support staff, usually as an Information Technology Specialist. The NSA designator is F6.

They worked out of State Department Annex 82 (SA 82) in Laurel, MD about 3 minutes from Jon's house. If you left SA 82 to go to NSA at Ft. Meade, you did an SDR with at least 2 cover stops. Going back, you took a different route. Same with Langley or any other spook place. There was a massive warehouse on the back end that housed a lot of antennas (those 4-5m satellite antennas with their pedestals take up some space.) The front end of the building and grounds was built to look like an embassy. There was a decent gym and locker room set up. There was a lab with an anechoic chamber for testing as well as live antennas on the roof to collect test shots to a controlled segment of a cell tower A-bis interface on the Capitol Technology University (of which half the classes were for NSA cyber curriculum). The basement were full mock ops of server rooms with all the same processors as in use OCONUS down in the basement. You connected the gear together with old school patch panels like you saw in the 50s telecom rooms.

There was a bunch of technical training to be certified as an operator/engineer. Some of it was done at a Raytheon cover facility called "Crossroads" in Fair Lakes, VA. Jon had to fit all that in with the required weapons, tradecraft and driving course to be qualified as a deployer in a war zone. His first task was to get ready to go out the door and deploy and serve in a collection site. Weapons qual was done at Camp Peary (you know, the 'Armed Forces Experimental Training Activity')— where they would train on and be issued iron sight stock Glocks and M4s. In this capacity, Jon was not a super cool shooter door kicker in any regard, his job was amongst mostly geeks and chick analysts/linguists doing the collection work, but they had the right and some training to defend themselves.

After weapons qual, you did get to do the Crash and Bang course, officially called OPSC (Officer Personal Security Course). There each student drove a race course, a very specific timed event, some crazy scenarios where you had to back up in a jersey wall channeled course with 90 degree turns in reverse to 'to get off the X'; they drove regular cars downtown Williamsburg to see if they could pick up a tail by learning how to do SDRs for those who had not previously; and 24/7 were always looking out for an 'attack' or road ambush; they drove another race course in SUVs and pickups that had varying road coverings, loose gravel, mud, dirt, impaired asphalt. Because it was under a UW type scenario, students had to check the vehicle they used to get to the classrooms, barracks, mess hall, ranges for IEDs and bombs because it was a semi-permissive environment scenario.

The culmination exercise was driving on the secondary roads throughout Peary at night where there were roadblocks, an OPFOR in terrorist garb where the right answer was there was no way out of the situation alive without ramming the cars parked nose to nose blocking the way. It was thorough preparation to go into hostile territory. All this and a paycheck, too. Additionally, they had med training at a site in McLean, VA (GSW, sucking chest wounds, tourniquet application, tension pneumothorax treatment) and on how best to deploy the issued blow out kit when needed.

Jon very much wanted to go to Sulaymaniyah, IQ or Yemen, but instead went to Herat, AFG. His rationale was simple— proximity to Iranian IRGC-QF operations that threated stability in the region. His fellow deployers went to Dulles in a bus, went onto the tarmac in a back area, were met by 'Customs' people who rubberstamped us out of the US and got on board a chartered aircraft called the Airbridge. They landed in Kabul, taxied over to the Kabul Airport Compound (KAC) where there were barracks, chow hall and a movie theatre and you were processed for your flight to your site and were issued a weapons and assault vest. As part of his in processing, Jon had to register a new call sign. Serpico was being used, so he chose 'Riptide', a magical sword from the Rick Riordan book he was reading.

He went not to the Herat consulate (which got rocketed nearly once a week), but to an 'annex' that was 100% an Agency safe house. All doors and doorframes were steel, there were ballistic blankets covering every window, there was an actual aircraft FLIR on a telescoping pole like a periscope on the roof for night use only, a rifleman ready to shoot the engine block of any vehicle coming into the front gate, a sally port for the back gate food deliveries. The outside perimeter wall that surrounded the compound was guarded by 'vetted' local Afghans who had an entire house to themselves inside the wire. There was an inner layer guard force to watch the Afghans, all US guys with combat experience. What happened at Chapman in 2010 was not going to happen here.

There was a small chow hall which was open 24/7. There was a chicken, beef, lamb dish of some varying sort every dinner, lots of variety. The cook for the first several weeks was South African and he made a South African dinner for Christmas. Cook wasn't quite accurate; he was really a chef—he was superb! Jon's initial task was to obtain and bring on his infil an injector to marinate a turkey that the analyst, Bait Caster, was going to deep fry for Christmas. He accomplished that mission and was declared a hero from day one.

Jon met his special intelligence (the 'SI') team in the chow hall and in a very pleasant surprise, saw an old friend, Kim Taylor from their training days at the Idaho National Laboratory. Kim walked straight up to him and smiled, "Hi! I'm the SI OIC, Cocoa. Haven't seen you in a while. Welcome!"

Jon couldn't help but notice true names or pseudos' were not exchanged. OK. He was incredibly pleased to see she obviously had kept in the game and was maybe moving up in her career. She would later privately confide she had married Jason in real life, and that Jason, a former Navy SEAL, was a paramilitary officer in Ground Branch. He returned a salutation with equal gusto, "Hi, all. I'm Riptide."

It was a small team. Cocoa introduced their linguist, Gondi, and their analyst Baitcaster. Gondi was quite an interesting sort— he spoke Farsi, Pashtu, Dari, French and of course, English. He had been born in Tehran and as a child, fled the insanity of the Islamic Republic with his mother to Turkmenistan. He eventually made his way to the US, became a citizen and had qualified for a security clearance at NSA.

Gondi said, "While you are here with us, I'd offer you join us at the fire pit every other Wednesday night. I prepare a meal for us and a guest of my choice. Will you join us?"

Gondi was very formal in speech, but apparently quite a prankster in the house. After Riptide received his initiation, he learned perhaps too late that Gondi translated roughly as 'meatball' in Persian.

Although Riptide had a desk and workstation in the server room (very noisy and not a lot of space), every day he was on the roof in the shelter (roof top shelter, RTS, a radio transparent hootch in which antennas and cable runs were terminated then meandered circuitously 126' down to the processors in the basement/SCIF). He did a great deal of environmental survey, sweeping the parabolic antennas and horn feeds to find a fat, juicy large capacity signal. The antenna was connected to a spectrum analyzer that graphically showed when you were at the highest signal strength, then you started loading up the modulation applications to see what kind of signal you had (QPSK, 8PSK, 128 QAM, etc.).

On the compound were, of course, 5-6 case officers, the Chief of Base/ Dep COB (DCOBs call sign was 'Q', an old, black former SF NCO) and the Global Response Staff (GRS). One of the GRS team leads call sign was 'Hondo' who was a former 1st Group NCO who was from New Hampshire. Basically, GRS recons the route to and from a personal meet (PM, or just 'meet') site, where the case officer is exposed and linking up with a person betraying his host nation friends for money. That source is tasked to obtain and report information of interest and does so at great personal risk.

GRS gets the CO there and back to home base, maybe another SH or safe haven area where they can debrief, or whatever they do. A CO might meet with the source and say take this cell phone with you when you go to the mayor's party (the cell phone is an IMSI grabber wrapped up in a normal cell phone package). GRS' whole job is CO protection, whether it's a vehicle pick up (VPU) meet or whatever that CO needs. GRS might have a few teams backing up, depending on the situation, it might be only 2 guys. COs try to develop new sources, or they are handling a current case load, or both. It is not particularly exciting, but you can see where it might get hairy if things go sideways.

Hondo let Rip go out on a few VPU (vehicle pick up) runs. He really wasn't supposed to do that HUMINT shit—the F6ers are held to just their duties as SIGINT geeks unless in extremis. Cocoa broadly interpreted the normal rules as she knew full well Rip's other talents. Lots of operational things flow through embassies and bases. A telecom cable/fiber run from Iran ran along the border to Turkmenistan where there was a JPO (actually, now called RESOLUTE HYPERION) access point. The JPO/Ground Branch boys had to do some maintenance, and Jon asked to go along and hump up a fucking mountain the 70-pound sealed car batteries used for power. His final JPO mission was to provide security for a CIA geologist doing a soil sample to determine if the ground was diggable for another clandestine access outside a DynCorp compound at Islam Qaleh.

Only one pretty cool thing happened while he was there, and it was unusual for Herat where there was little to no serious terrorist activity. On 12 December, Baqui Mortezavi, an Iranian Republic Guard Corps—Quds Force (IRGC-QF) element 409 operative that was rooted out by Baitcaster searching one of the station's discovered PCM links. This was fortuitous beyond measure, an absolute needle in the haystack. Baitcaster figured out the Iranian's rough location, then COB brought in NDS-78, the Afghan National Defense Security wireless SIGINTers as the HN partners to fix and finish. The COB further sought the Marine MARSOC element to help by flying a Scan Eagle mini-drone out of Shindad Air Base to vehicle follow. After SSE, cell phones were brought to base to be 'ripped' forensically for further exploitation.

After a very short 4 months Jon said his farewells and returned to stateside, not a single shot fired, no one even had an accidental discharge.

Chapter 12

2012, Ft. Meade, Maryland

Over the last very satisfying years at SCS, Jon had completed tours of varying lengths to Jolo in the Philippines hunting Abu Sayyaf (ASG) and twice to Sana'a, Yemen. In both cases, he found ways to go 'outside the wire'. His OIC in the Philippines, Danny, was not quite as forgiving and tolerant as Cocoa, and he wrote Jon up. Jon was not in the least bit concerned. What *did* concern him, though, was the chatter they were hearing regarding the Houthis being supported by Iran, and how blatant at times that support was.

At his last stint in Sana'a, his relative seniority was recognized: he would spend the last 6-months of his mobilization tour as the OIC at the station. Even though he still a newbie within SCS circles, he was a lieutenant-colonel in the United States Army and had more than enough leadership experience. He did not campaign for this, it just happened. So, when it came time to return to the Yemen, he could write his own ticket as far as to what operations he could support. Personally.

There was a new Chief of Station now, so in his in brief, Jon gave the COS a short overview of his past experiences that might apply here. Naturally, Jon's JSOC pedigree and his drone build out activities came up, and the COS said, "So, we got a little problem over there across the border with Umm al Mehl, which hence we'll call Site 1. They seem to be taking some harassment mortar fire from our side of the border, so it's my problem just as much as Riyadh's."

Rip inquired, "How can I help, boss?"

COS continued, "We'd like a SI team to see if they can do some force protection, at least give some early warning so folks can get to shelter prior to an attack."

Rip offered, "Since I'm pretty familiar with the layout, let me take some equipment and a couple GRS guys in Land Rovers and extra fuel so we can check out the signals environment, lines of sight, and billeting availability, and I'll see if I can figure out the requirements and make a plan."

Now Rip had 'top cover' for his excursion. It was far out of his authority to do anything permanent, so in his cable to the NSA HQ folks, he made his request: "Please provide 2 PAX who are self-reliant, mature and able to live in austere conditions. They should be qualified on Glocks and M4s for commonality of ammo. They will receive protective vests with plates and Kevlar helmets upon arrival to Station. These personnel can come from MUSKATEER or even the SIGINT Squadron, as JSOC has equities, too. I'll leave those details to you. More to follow after site survey. Send me, Riptide."

Rip loaded up. In lieu of a GRS guy, he was lent an ex-SF State Department Diplomatic Security protective officer from the Regional Security Office (RSO) who was pals with an ex-SF GRS dude named Axel. Both Axel and Chuck hailed from 1st SFG(A) and had known each other for years. After many hours of driving and an uneventful border crossing, the ad hoc team arrived at Site 1. COS had greased the skids and they were well received.

Rip surveyed the base and recalled the long hours spent

conceiving its construction. 5 years – that's how long it took to line all this up: the funding lines and how it would flow unattributively, the coordination between the Saudi intelligence service, building out roads to this unforsaken hellhole, the heavy equipment chained down to lowboys and transported, the 30kw generators for power and the fuel for the flight line, everything. All that planning, all that detail, and although he was not there for execution, he had to admit a little pride in its birth.

No time for reminiscence, back on your heads, he thought. He built a little rapport, exchanged contact information, set up some gear to survey, made his assessments, bunked for the night, got up the next day and returned to base. Get it done. He was, after all, the OIC at Station and that is where his responsibilities lie.

The trip to Site 1 was Rip's only excursion for this trip to Yemen. That doesn't mean it was uneventful—there was a great deal of traffic and activity alluding to an array of unsavory alliances following the Arab Spring and portended to conflicts with strategic consequence across the Middle East.

Chapter 13

2013, Syria

A student of history, al-Tamimi read:

"The invasion of Busr b. Artat of Hijaz and Yemen was among the most savage looting of Mu›awiya. Mu›awiya had asked Busr to kill followers of Imam ‹Ali (a) wherever he found them. After some disputes in Iraq, supporters of ‹Uthman in Yemen rose up against ‹Ubayd Allah b. ‹Abbas, the governor of Yemen and asked Mu'awiya for help. Busr first went to Medina and Abu Ayyub alAnsari escaped from there because he did not have enough soldiers. Busr burnt Abu Ayyub›s house and forced people to give allegiance and appointed Abu Hurayra as the governor of the city. He then went to Mecca and Ta›if. He killed a group of Shi'a in Tabala. People escaped in fear of Busr. Busr arrested the wife and children of ‹Ubayd Allah b. ‹Abbas and beheaded his children. He then went to Najran and killed ‹Abd Allah b. ‹Abd al-Madan, the father-in-law of ‹Ubayd Allah. Then, Busr went to Yemen. Few of Shi›a made little resistance and many of them were killed. Busr beheaded 100 Shi›a of Iranian origin. He then moved towards Hadramut where it was said that many Shi›a were living. After Imam (a) heard about the invasions of Busr, sent Jariya b. Qudama with an army to follow him, but when he arrived in Mecca, Busr had left the city. It

88 is said that before Jariya arrived in Kufa, Imam 'Ali (a) had been martyred and so he gave allegiance to Imam al-Hasan (a) when he arrived in Kufa."

Such were the events of the al-Mughira Umayyad caliphate in the year 680 AD. A devout Shia, al-Tamimi spent a great deal of his time in nurturing his hatred and applying it to the violence he spread across the Middle East. Of course, there were times when allying with Sunni was convenient when advantageous for broader, strategic goals. Since the ties between Syria and Iran were vital, his efforts to support the Al Nusra Front (ANF) were convenient to fostering Syria's destruction of opposing forces to the Assad regime which was largely possible as the Obama administration had buried it's head in the sand and steadfastly ignored Assad's chemical attacks against his own citizens.

Still, as al-Tamimi was fostering strife in Aleppo, he was concurrently developing new networks in Yemen and considering if there were a way forward in Somalia. He was haunted by nightmares of his brother's deaths from when ne narrowly escaped in Abu Kamal; however, he was equally confident more American blood would flow red in the desert sand.

Rachel Howard, aka Cocoa, was leaving her rental in Frederick, Maryland for the long drive to Langley. Her career was indeed on the ascent as she had recently accepted the position as a Branch chief in the Air Branch of the Special Activities Division of CIA. The general thrust of her operations heavily leaned towards drone operations, although some of her time was allocated to other airframes and as a Contracting Officer's Representative (COR), she was obligated to participate in aircraft modifications by Sierra Nevada Corporation completed at Hagerstown about an hour away. Her office was a short drive away in Ft. Detrick where her cover for status was as a staff officer in the 21st Signal Brigade, but she made the slog down 270 to Langley at least once a week.

More often than not, she was a geographical bachelorette as her husband, Dan was nearly continuously deployed for at least 6 weeks at a pop. Dan and Rachel would reunite at their home in McLean on weekends when he returned form his TDYs all over the globe. Rachel was to a degree jealous, but with a 4-year-old about to start school soon, one of them had the blessings of responsibilities beyond the Agency. These meetings in Langley were often tedious, but she used them as a platform to gather perspective on how her operations provided insight to policy makers. She had access, of course, to CWE in the SCIF at Ft. Detrick, but found she just didn't have the time to go through the volumes of intelligence reports that clogged its databases and it was always good to build rapport and network.

Rachel had developed a small cadre of Directorate of Intelligence (DI) analysts to whom she could go for briefings. These threat briefings were global and focused on not just the individual pieces but how North Korea, Iran, Russia, Cuba and China may be woven into a quilt of greater design. The nodes where the connections enjoined were of particular interest.

Jon Prescott had landed on his feet with a new job after his mobilization tour with the Army. He continued exploiting his organizational knowledge of NSA in which he had made inroads with a defense contractor called L3 Communications. Jon was particularly pleased with his offer letter, not so much as to his salary, but he had a health and dental package, something he had not had as an independent contractor and had not fully taken advantage of while on active duty orders. The molar that surely was an impending root canal needed tending to after years of neglect.

In an ironic twist, for this contract, L3 Communications had partnered with a telecom giant called Level 3 Communications, and although their core competencies were quite different, initially as a newbie Jon would attribute the wrong L3 to a task that fell under the rubric of the Special Source Operations division. The prime of the contract, to which he referred as 'his L3' was the systems integrator of the contract team, and the contract had three regional thrusts, of which Jon's interest was as a lead systems engineer on the East Africa Team.

Jon's career path was anything but a straight line; it was circuitous, and although there were logical off shoots, he had returned to a skillset he had acquired with the JPO in 1998. Based on the many commercial consortiums competing to build out undersea fiber communications systems connecting the Middle East, eastern Africa and Southeast Asia, Jon would assist the SSO in planning and building out sensitive technical collections nodes in a deliberate manner to span the area of interest. He was also pleased that this sole source contract was an anomalous 5 year with options gig. Since he was exceedingly aware of the laborious HUMINT constructs into which they would rely to enable the technical constructions of this operation, he strapped in for what he knew would be long, long journey with setbacks and minor triumphs of equal measure.

Chapter 14

2014, Annapolis Junction

Jon worked on a small planning team mostly comprised of NSA engineers, some of whom were Air Force or Navy officers. The initial task was to identify opportunities, and then, based on relationships with either host nation government or telecom service provider, make some design choices as to what was doable both on a cost and time basis; layered on to that variable, a particular eye on what HUMINT networks were already in place deserved equal consideration. The team had already made one rudimentary decision—Camp Lemonnier or its proximate facilities in Djibouti would continue serving the EASSY cable system, to which they would examine how best to approach the landing site in Tanzania due in 2016.

Jon had access to NSAnet, the secure IT system to which everyone working there with the right clearances had access, but he augmented the data with his research of online tech publications unique to the telecom world. One of his favorite was www.submarinecablemap.com; it was a favorite of his because they had fantastic graphics from which he could augment what could be a pretty dull and dry briefing. Today was the day the team would brief the branch chief Dennis, and Jon set the framework by announcing, "Morning, Boss. I'll set the mood with an overview, and then the good Captain and Lieutenant will get into the mission analysis details, some assumptions and our recommendations."

"First thing, sir, we'd like to bring you up to speed on current operations, the installation of a PacketLight PL-1000RO ROADM switching unit at the Djibouti Data Center. First slide. Through some host nation skullduggery via CIA, the switch installation is complete and fully tested. The Agency folks did a great job developing some assets that could make this happen. The next phase is connecting to our facilities at the airport:

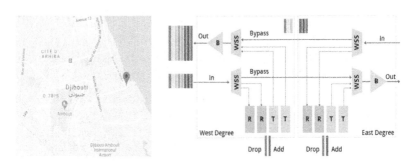

As a reminder, the switching unit's function is dual purpose, right from their website info or brochures:

- ROADMs offer the flexibility to add wavelengths or easily change their destination.

- In addition, they can be managed remotely, providing full control and monitoring over the entire high capacity infrastructure.

- Mirroring/Replicating data to Disaster Recovery Sites'

In both cases, we hear everything that transits the network!"

To this announcement followed a polite smattering of clapping and hooting. It was a start. The technical work was not the long pole in the tent, the identification and recruiting of some host nation technicians who would look the other way was what held this project up. This was to be a long game of patience if they were going to succeed in a task of this size.

"OK, let's roll with slide 2 and get right into future operations. This is the PEACE cable system," he elaborated. The slide was projected onto the screen built into Dennis' conference room wall:

"Sir, you may notice that the 'Ready For Service' or RFS of the system is Q1 2021, but PEACE is already sending active traffic between Points of Presence or POPs in Egypt. Other cable landing sites or CLS are in various stages of completion along its path as is the state of the submarine cable lay. To provide for some additional fail safes, we can leverage other infrastructure in place at DJ other than the data center, and we are looking at Mombasa, Mogadishu, and Karachi as attack points of interest.

"I have completely forgotten the source where I read this, but

I'll just quote the article," he reached into his notes and recited:

> 'The PEACE subsea cable is apparently positioned to promote business interests of China in Africa. Starting from Pakistan (landing in Gwadar and Karachi), expectedly with terrestrial extension to China, it lands on Djibouti and Kenya. It will understandably provide shortest submarine cable route from China to Africa. Further it is led by Huawei and China-ASEAN Information Harbor Co. Ltd. and does not seem to have any telecom provider as consortium member. The scale of operation and investment that China has lined up for Africa is to some extent evident from their participation in subsea cable builds.'

Captain Murdoch took the center stage for a moment. "Dennis, we're a little concerned that Huawei is so intertwined into this consortium – it's to be expected as the land lines will eventually make their way across Pakistan right into China. We'll have a lot less options with the routing and optical processing gear— for sure, it'll be Huawei." Inwardly, Jon winced as this was probably obvious to the GS-14 branch chief who had been at NSA for 22 years. Also, Jon would try to delicately let the good Air Force captain know that addressing the branch chief with such informality should probably only be done after a great deal of daily rapport and trust had been built.

Jon continued, "Not an insignificant challenge. Slide 3 please. Same deal, the DARE-1 RFS is in the 2020 time frame, but it's transit points are equally compelling:"

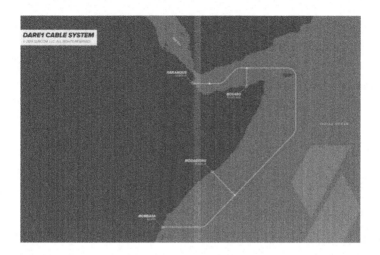

"DARE-1 doesn't particularly hit any new ground. In fact, it is redundant to PEACE's CLS sites at DJ, Mogadishu, Mombasa, and Bossaso, but it holds an exceptionally large advantage in that, unlike PEACE, the infrastructure is American. Each site is serviced with Ciena optical equipment in the SLTE and on top of that, the cable laying contract falls under SubCom with whom we already have a strong relationship," he stated, "We may yet be able to do some cross connects between the DARE-1 and PEACE nodes to get sufficient or alternative access points."

Lieutenant Hogan, generally quiet and a wall flower at briefings, managed to offer, "I might be able to liaise with SubCom to develop efforts if required." Hogan didn't talk about his service as a submariner due to the compartments related to intel collection conducted by the Navy's submarine attack boats. They were an awfully close hold community. SubCom's fleet was a surface fleet, but SubCom and Oceaneering were at the top of food chain as far as deep water Remotely Operated Vehicles (ROVs) were concerned.

Jon finished his end of the briefing with, "Sir, so far, we have identified the immediate attack points. We recommend immediately bolstering the CLS vicinity DJ. One, the optical equipment such as the branching units and repeaters need upgrading. We have relationships both with Djibouti Telecom and Golis Telecom and can 'help' with upgrading undersea repeaters to erbium doped fiber amplifiers to increase the optical signal-to-noise ratio (OSNR), not to mention slide in some special routing software, nudge, nudge, wink, wink.

Two, we'll have to figure out a means to intercept traffic as it feeds into or out of Pakistan. That's our number two priority as it'll require the longest lead time to account for what we assess as likely Chinese counterintelligence efforts to protect data enroute to or from China. Gwadar is the deep-water port on the border of Iran that China built from which the railways and underground cables cut all the way up to Islamabad. Karachi might be a better target as it is far more frenetic and commercial in nature and serves a larger market by population.

Three, Mogadishu and Bossaso afford the greatest capacity due to clustering of the DARE-1 and PEACE lines, but for now, Somalia is pretty much the wild west. Those are on a relative back burner due to risk. Tanzania and Kenya, relative to East Africa have calm and rosy dispositions, so Mombasa is the top card in the deck and Dar es Salaam should also be considered to augment the DJ station of the EASSY network. Lastly, way downstream 2AFRICA will have an RFS of 2024, but the planned site at Nacala would also have regional connection to Mozambique."

Dennis brought the briefing to a conclusion with a preliminary decision. With no prevarication, he instructed, "Some great work, folks. At my level, I can authorize immediate refurbishment and technology upgrades at DJ. Jon, please work out a schedule and the costs. We can at least get that started, send out a PDSS to DJ; L.T., you are in charge, I think even contractors can wear an ACU uniform with the right patches there, so military cover, Jon, you tag along since you have familiarity with the base. It would appear we have the bones of a CONOP."

Chapter 15

2015, Nairobi

The SSO East Africa Team in Annapolis Junction had also briefed the project, now called ELIXER, to higher level leadership in both NSA and CIA. The team had begun the CIA briefs to folks in DS&T, specifically the Office of Technical Collection, and the branch chief there, Alison Kraus, had recommended a further briefing at Langley to Glenn Gaffney the head of the S&T. Gaffney was fully on board, directed a full-time technical operations officer be assigned to the project as a lead engineer and further advanced the project by simply picking up the phone and calling a counterpart in the NCS. In that brief call his counterpart secured the COS in Nairobi as being the central node for implementation as well as three operations officers and a targeting officer to base out of the embassy there and roam the AO to recruit the necessary assets and oversee the HUMINT end of ELIXER.

Although at this juncture DJ was a more secure base and would serve as the warehouse and logistical hub from which to stage gear, Kenya would eventually be more centrally located as the full extent of ELIXER matured in the build out of its operational matrix. Dennis and Jon both flew to Jomo Kenyatta International Airport and were picked up by some junior staff for transport to the embassy in the Gigiri suburb that is Kenya's largest expatriate community.. Dennis provided a more detailed brief to the COS who asked they stay for a few days to work out support plans and timelines. In the course of the day, the Regional Security Officer gave them a threat brief for the Nairobi area during their TDY here. Jon had heard this before—stay out of the Deep Sea slum section of town.

The COS was a pretty busy man, but he took the time to have a coffee with the TDYers and the assigned supporting team, "Dennis, I'd like you to meet the team lead, in this case the targeting officer Jill Monroe, and our operations officers that will create regional access opportunities for ELIXER. They are, left to right as seated, Phil, Dave and Jaylen. Jill, I'll leave it to you."

With that, the gaggle left the COS' office and entered the pre-coordinated conference room in the Bubble. Jill began, "Well, Dennis, Jon we're all very excited to get down to it. I've already done some research and understand we have past operational contacts at Djibouti Telecom, Safaricom and the University of Nairobi Security Department in Kenya, Cybernet in Pakistan, and Golis Telecom in Somalia."

Dennis reiterated the general priorities and asked Jill if they were sequenced right. Jill responded, "Well I think we can put our toe in the water to develop Golis in Bossaso even now as a long lead time, and for that Jaylen will work that issue as well as Dar es Salaam. For the time being, we will put Mogadishu on the back burner. It's the focal point of Al Shabab terror activity, the rest of the country is not too bad."

"Do you have any other recommendations on sequencing the technical framework we've devised so far?", Jon inquired. Dennis nodded in affirmation as he was thinking now was the time to make adjustments to the plan.

Jill carried on, "I think we have to focus more on Pakistan as that may offer some challenges. Dave will work that as well as the lower hanging fruit here initially at Kenya. Dave already has someone in Mombasa in Safaricom that's assisting with some SCS efforts as well as a pretty good rapport with the JSOC HUMINTers in Manda Bay. They may have some insights into at least southern Somalia. He can liaise there and see if they can help with applicable contacts. That leaves Phil to assist the build out at DJ and work the very far downstream Nacala landing site for 2AFRICA.

Jon, I understand you have a military background. It might be useful if you go to Manda Bay with Dave tomorrow."

Jon and Dave got up at zero dark thirty and flew into the recently refurbished airstrip on Lama Island. In 2012, the station got an upgrade with a host of improvements completed and under construction at the time including a new dining facility, extra fuel storage tanks, a new well and expanded water storage, and new power generators. Even those recent upgrades showed some jungle rot. They made their way to the ops compound that was centered around a small house that had once been in shambles—broken roof, smashed walls, trees growing through the floor—but was now, after several deployments of special warfare personnel, structurally sound with a new red roof and a fresh coat of white paint.

Jon did indeed see an old colleague, a graduate of the NAR course in Nevada still going by the call sign 'Cuda. It turns out 'Cuda was a ST6 senior chief who gregariously welcomed Jon with a loud, "Serpico, you're a good lookin' man, mate, don't think I haven't noticed. How's it hangin'?"

'Cuda was also the HARC chief as well, but had only been in

country for a month. "'Cuda, I don't know if you've met Dave, he'll be working some special programs out of 'Nobi and might need some help," Jon explained.

"Yeah, dude, pleasure. My predecessor Loop briefed me you were a POC in our transition as well as the network he had established or had been passed down to him. I got my hands full handling my current case load as I am one PAX short in the shop." 'Cuda commenced crushing Dave's hand with his ham sized hands.

Over a beer, 'Cuda and Jon told war stories about training, back when it was hard. The three then brought in the team leader and J3X to give a sanitized broad overview and to just lay down a place holder if there were any opportunities with which the Manda Bay AFO team could aid. For situational awareness and with a request that the information was relayed back to the COS, 'Cuda regaled the small group with an update on potential targets and plans to action those objectives. Although a very sporadic long shot, one of those targets was Objective Dawa.

Chapter 16
2016-2018, Pakistan

The Pakistan portion of ELIXER was complicated enough to earn its own unofficial nickname, HEADACHE. There were two very big links in the wet end of the chain, one of which that required the unwitting cooperation of the Intergovernmental Oceanographic Commission (IOC). The general thrust was for the Agency, through a National Oceanographic and Atmospheric Agency (NOAA) cover, to offer to add hurricane monitoring sensors on the existing sea level monitoring ocean observing platforms offshore of Karachi. A great deal of money was exchanged, particularly a grant for scientific 'R&D'. This sensor would not infringe on the station's resources; the evacuation of the data would be two-fold, a satellite uplink and a fiber optic cable of its own. The current capability and data set on the ocean platform looked like:

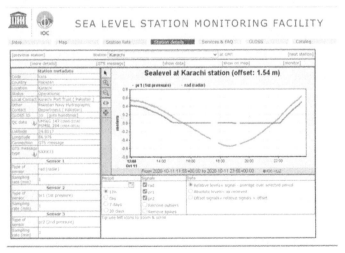

The second link in the chain was how to power the remote operated sensors and comms infrastructure on the ocean platform as well as a specially modified branch unit to be emplaced when other conditions were set. Of these two elements, this was logistically challenging, but doable. It entailed making a deal with a government with whom the US and Britain in particular had solid relations: Oman. To give an idea of exactly how much money flowed through oil interests in the Middle East, there was a gentleman who literally owned his own cable (TW1) connecting Oman to Pakistan: His Excellency Dr Omar Abdul Mone'm Yousuf Al Zawawi of the Sultanate of Oman. Through the Transworld Associates CLS, the US then laid cable from the Power Feeding Equipment (PFE) to the ocean platform.

Lieutenant Hogan was becoming the star of the show; he had a unique skillset that was nearly a perfect match for HEADACHE. As the ocean monitoring platform data was managed by the Pakistan Navy Hydrographic Department, Hogan added some nautical value to the IOC coordination affected by Dave. More importantly, his knowledge of submarine activities and boats is what made the entire endeavor possible. In fact, he came up with the idea in the first place.

While the sensor container was being barged out to the ocean monitoring platform, SSN-23, the USS Jimmy Carter was steaming to a loiter point midway between the platform and where the Y-junction splitter divided the mainland cable from the Gulf of Aden to the CLS at Gwadar and the CLS at Karachi.

On board it had a modified repeater that not only amplified the optical signal of the PEACE branch to Karachi but duplicated it and sent the mirrored signal and all its content along the cable to the platform.

Although Huawei Marine manufactured all the cables, repeaters, SLTEs and PFEs for the PEACE cable, they outsourced the cable laying and survey operations to E-marine, the principal provider of submarine cable solutions in the Middle East. They outsourced this vital task to save on CAPEX outlays. Huawei Marine had originally partnered with the British company Global Marine Systems, into which MI6 still had agents with placement and access (PAA). In her nearly continual loop of searching for targets to be exploited, Jill Monroe had located one of those agents ported at Gwadar on the CS Maram, a cable ship attached by E-marine solely to the PEACE cable project.

Once all the hurricane monitoring sensors and cable were laid and tested, the agent at Gwadar inserted a USB fob into a specific computer port while the CS Maram was in the port. On the fob was a virus that rendered all software used to chart efficient cable lays inoperable. Without the software, the ship was useless as far as doing its job. Shortly after, a fishing trawler cut the cable of the branch leading into Karachi. The software on the Y-junction splitter switched all traffic and power from Karachi off and to the Gwadar branch. That process looks somewhat like this:

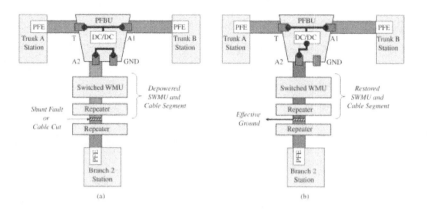

Since the CS Maram was out of commission, Huawei had to find a cable ship in the area that could do the job. They found one, the CS Resolute, a US flagged vessel from SubCom that was steaming west from Mumbai. When the *Resolute* was close enough to shore where the cable fault was suspected to be based on impedances monitored at the CLS, a handful of Chinese 'technicians' would helicopter out, board, and 'offer technical assistance and translation.' Read: we do not trust you Americans and will monitor everything you do.

Meanwhile, the USS Carter had reached its destination and brought the platform's length of cable inside a special chamber in which the optical technicians where the men then do the work while the sub clandestinely hugged the ocean floor. In this chamber--called a jointing room--crews work on the delicate fibers. When repairing a broken cable, cable companies generally lift one end of the rupture to the surface and into the jointing room, splice in a new length of cable, then lift the other end of the rupture and repeat the process. The USS Carter was purpose built in the 80's to perform this type of operation, and to do it underwater, unseen.

Not to put all eggs in one basket, and since they had relationships at Cybernet, the team was conducting a study on risk vs. reward in trying to mirror access at Cybernet points of presence, also in Karachi. They were unsure where the POP was that would service the capacity screaming over the PEACE cable, but the concept was worth exploring. An image capturing the general optical architecture looked like:

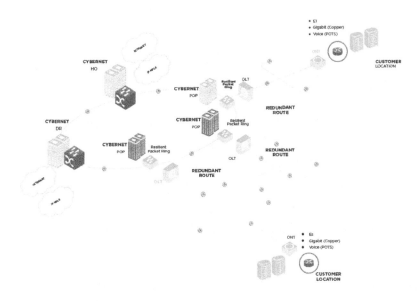

Since the entire wet plant operation took nearly two years, the POP option was set on the backburner for now. The team had to take solace in the fact they had pulled off a major operation where compromise had been a pretty damn high probability. The actual payoff of the eventual data acquisition was still to be determined and they still had the rest of the network projects to manage. The victory dance was quite short, but vigorous. Gotta take the good moments when they come.

Chapter 17

2018, Malawi

An extensive rare earth element (REE) mining project had been up and running in Malawi for a few years and was beginning to produce the ores with efficiency and profitability. At the surface, the corporation leading the charge was a Canadian firm called Mkango. In an online publication called ShareTalk, Alexander Lemon, the president of Mkango provided a status that the firm was completing 59 drill holes at Songwe Hill as well as touting the impact of the company's partnership with Talaxis Limited, which had pumped in about £7 million into the feasibility study.

MiningReview.com, another online trade publication reported that Talaxis had entered a MoU with Chinalco Guangxi Nonferrous Rare Earth Development Co to further their cooperation in sourcing, development, and production of rare earths. Daniel Mamadou, Talaxis executive director commented that, "This agreement with (state-run Aluminum Corp of China) Chinalco represents the potential for a significant offtake contract in the growing rare earths sector. Our strategic long-term collaboration with one of Asia's leading metals companies will help to further strengthen Talaxis' position as the supply partner of choice in the technology metals industry."

In other words, Jon thought, the entire project was a project run by and benefiting China but with a Canadian veneer. Further research brought him other insights, particularly of scope. Clearly, those 59 drill holes covered a large patch of ground:

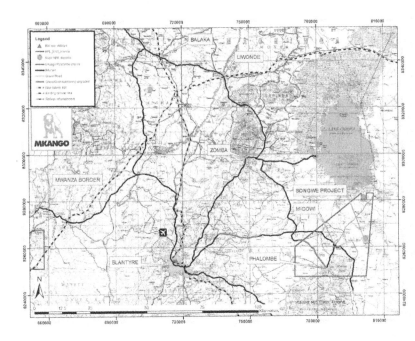

The primary purpose of the ELIXER project was to determine China's influence in the continent of Africa, yet a great deal of activity was occurring while the undersea cable collection sites were being put into place. Jon believed a great deal of collection was being dropped, and he was beginning to think a terrestrial effort should be initiated, at least until all the shoreline cable access were fully operational.

He put together a graphic so he could envision a way to attack this problem:

Right now, Malawi's only access to the big pipes from the sea was via the fiber-optic network SimbaNET that was launched by MTL in May 2016, and established a connection between the capital, Lilongwe, and Tanzania. Jaylen was making significant headway in getting a mirror CLS site constructed in Dar es Salaam, but the EASSY cable was not due to be connected and tested for a few months. SimbaNET was connected to the SEACOM cable system and was not on the target list due to cost constraints. Still, it is likely valuable traffic would flow through Lilongwe and downstream to Zomba where the US had a consulate.

From a report by www.freedomhouse.org, Jon extracted a few

nuggets of data pertinent to the problem space:

- Malawi has a total of six fiber gateways to the SEACOM cable landings, three each through MTL and the Electricity Supply Corporation of Malawi Limited (ESCOM).

- Mobile phone services are offered by three providers—Airtel Malawi, TNM, and Access Communications. The industry is dominated by a de facto duopoly of Airtel Malawi and TNM

- The government requires the use of official documents to register SIM cards, undermining ability of Malawians to communicate anonymously via mobile phones. SIM card registration is mandatory in Malawi, as stipulated by the 2016 Communications Act

- Both Airtel Malawi and TMN have invested in LTE to improve data services

- Regulator uses USF to install mobile towers in rural areas, to be leased to Airtel Malawi and MTL for a fee

The 2AFRICA cable into Nacala would clearly fix most of the issue, but the RFS for that was 2023, so no help there for the time being. Possibly because that was such a far away target, the operations officer on the team from CIA just wasn't aggressive enough in setting up the necessary HUMINT asset network to facilitate a smooth transition and have first class penetration into the required service providers. That was bad enough, but even DJ had missed IOC and FOC milestones for what was thought to be the easy slam dunk of the entire project. They did indeed have a fully compromised SLTE servicing the

DARE-1 cable in DJ, but that had slipped the schedule by over 9 months.

Jon knew what the problem was, but as a contractor and not a blue badger in a leadership position, he knew it was out of his place to directly solve. The operations officer Phil was teamed up with Captain Murdoch, the spring butt Air Force officer who, incongruently, was fully qualified as a Junior Officer Cryptologic Career Program (JOCCP) graduate, the NSA's premier, tailor-made curriculum to develop officers for future leadership positions within the Cryptologic Community. JOCCP grads were normally the cream of the crop. Between Dave and Murdoch, installations were lagging. Jon would bring this up to Dennis, and frankly, recommend both be replaced.

When he considered the amount of time that had elapsed, the broader issue that was apparent was that there probably needed to be an effort to augment the seaborne collection with an equally intense terrestrial collection strategy. That, too, he would recommend to Dennis, but he had a preliminary band-aid solution to the Malawi focus. MTL had it's largest data center in Lilongwe due to the termination of the SimbaNET fiber optic cable there. Malawi was one the world's poorest countries, and Jon was confident Dave could convince some corrupt MTL technician with enough backsheesh that installing a PacketLight PL-1000RO ROADM for a robust disaster recovery solution was a really good idea.

Since the mobile phone was so regulated and sporadic in the rural areas, the best the team could do for now was to coordinate with the SCS team in the consulate in Zomba to focus collection to calls related to the Mkango Songwe dig.

The SCS folks should also get a Chinese interpreter on staff to field calls in at least Mandarin or Cantonese. Jon could help grease the skids if need be as he was an alum. For that matter, Dennis was too, although not in the Field Operations Office (FOO), like Jon. Dennis had spent most of his career in the Technology Directorate (TD), but his stint at SCS was in the Field Engineering Office (FEO). Jon was sure that Dennis could make it happen.

Chapter 18
2018-2019, Somalia

Jaylen's time on the project was often spent travelling to Africa from Dulles in Virginia, and he concluded it was wasted time, so he requested orders to base out of Nairobi. The bureaucracy in Langley churned and there was a bean counter somewhere in the bowels wringing her hands, but eventually his request was approved. He was actually well received by the COS in 'Nobi because Jaylen could be tasked for a few more cases to be fully utilized. The Station had become the hub of not only the expanding ELIXER program, but for East Africa as well.

Shabab militants in early 2019 had assaulted a hotel-shopping complex in Nairobi, Kenya, killing at least 21 people, including a police officer. Six years earlier, masked gunmen stormed the upscale Westgate Shopping Mall in the Kenyan capital, in a rampage that killed at least 67 people. Jaylen, whose father had been born in Sierra Leone 1960 and immigrated to the US as a teen, was more than aware of the cycle of violence that often gripped Africa and he wanted to help in creating some semblance of stability.

The targeting officer, Jill, was always working and finding good, well, targets. From a Bangor Daily News article, she found a young man who had grown up in Somalia and had embraced America with all his heart. Abdi Moalim was the rare sort who fully accepted American culture and integrated himself with gusto; he assimilated America as his home and his destiny, to the extent, according to the article, "Since he 115 was a child,

Moalim always saw the United States as a beacon of hope. He watched old presidential addresses on YouTube such as Ronald Reagan's famous "shining city on the hill" speech. But now that he's here, and about to become a fully franchised citizen, he knows the American Dream is more complicated than that."

Jaylen had 'accidently' run into Abdi at a horse farm in Yarmouth, struck up a conversation, then ended up sharing a coffee, which he took with plenty of sugar, but no milk. Abdi had noted Jaylen's coffee fetish and joked that he should try Ethiopian beans, they are the best, he exclaimed. This 'casual encounter' led to the two meeting at Arabica Coffee on Free Street in the Old Port area of Portland. Abdi also introduced a South African blend of a reddish tea called Rooibos to the mix. As was the custom in Ethiopia, it is impolite to retire until you have consumed at least three cups, as the third round is considered to bestow a blessing. In the conversation, Abdi mentioned his brother was later allowed to immigrate to Canada, and the two were recently reunited in Toronto after more than five years apart.

After a few months, Jaylen eventually made his pitch. What Jaylen was looking for was someone who could, on occasion, travel to Somalia or Kenya, make introductions and to procure rental vehicles, apartments, commercial property, that sort of thing. Of course, Abdi would receive a generous stipend, even help with capitalizing business ventures in Somalia if Abdi would like to return to his homeland.

Jaylen fully enjoyed his time in Maine. It was a beautiful state, the summers so pleasant along the coast where the breeze carried the salty scent of the sparkling, clean Atlantic. He had watched the season's change to Autumn with its golden birch, the occasional ruby red Japanese maple, against the backdrop of the omni-present cone laden pines. Now the air turned to chill with even more crisp mornings trumpeting the harbinger of the inevitable winter.

This was one case of many. He went from the comfort of a pleasant Maine early summer afternoon to the blast furnace of Bossaso, Somalia where they received less than a ½ inch of rain a year and it was over 92 degrees between March and October. Just as his travels were circuitous, the path to fertile recruiting grounds was equally nonlinear, yet sometimes fortuitous. Through Abdi, Jaylen became aware of the Somali diaspora in Scandinavia, and then the Danish branch of the Scandinavian Somali Network; this led to his awareness of an al-Shabaab terrorist rehab program where defectors were reintegrated into useful lives from a house called Serendi.

Serendi was to be the focal point of defector rehabilitation coordination where a group of anthropologists conducting high-risk ethnography field research study how and why Somalis were radicalized. Just as important as it's placement into Mogadishu, was that its deputy project manager, Halima had already been recruited and was on the lookout for candidates of a family member or friend of a candidate with any kind of connection to P&O Ports, which is owned by the Government of Dubai, or to consortium members Djibouti Telecom, Somtel and Telkom Kenya. Jill's research had 'dredged up' a little factoid of potential opportunity: that the $30M project of modernizing the port facilities in Bossaso would involve building a 450m quay and a 5 hectare back up area, dredging to a depth of 12m with reclamation work using dredge spoil. There was also to be major investment in an IT and Terminal Operating System (TOS), mobile harbor cranes and container handling equipment.

While the port at Bossaso was being re-jiggered and its infrastructure built from scratch, the inbound DARE-1 cable was doing to have some of its own modernization to upgrade the two-pair cable to 40 channels of 300 Gbps DWDM technology.

The technical approach to gaining access to the DARE-1 was to involve the supply interdiction of a cable repeater and branching unit assembly that would be replaced with modified equipment that had software permitting rerouting of data packets. Once again, Lieutenant Hogan was called on to liaise with the underwater community to a marine route survey to understand the conditions of the seabed where the cable was to be laid and to design a cable route based on the achieved information by the survey. The marine route survey consists of conducting a geophysical survey by means of acoustic sounding methods and a geotechnical survey using sub-bottom profiling. The survey then generates the Straight Line Diagram as a graphical representation of the route position list in order to instruct the factory to produce the submersible plants. The products of these efforts look like:

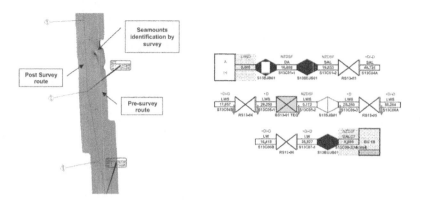

Whilst Mogadishu itself was still a little hinky and nastily dangerous, Jaylen oftentimes travelled to or based out of the Soviet built airbase in Baledogle where there was a significant African Union Mission in Somalia (AMISOM) force influencing the Lower Shebelle region. He had spent his time on ELIXER wisely and had created a logistical and operational network to carry out the technical tasks, although the Mogadishu project was maybe 3 months behind schedule, and that was due to threat situations he could not control. For the most part, he and his superiors were content with the progress in Somalia.

Chapter 19

January 3, 2020, Ft. Meade

As with any day at ELIXER, Jon ran through his morning routine and got to work early. He was typically the first one in and seated at his desk by 7:00 AM, having already drank a 12-ounce cup of Dunkins when others started filing in, tales of the Beltway and route 32 traffic the topic of discussion. The Commute. Jon hated talking about The Commute and zoned out on his Early Bird reading.

The day began with an ops brief to Dennis. Since the previous Air Force Captain had moved on to IAD, a great deal of progress had been made at DJ. Likewise, with Dar as Salaam. The Karachi and Mombasa nodes had been Full Operational Capacity (FOC) for over 9 months, and DJ and Bossaso were at IOC. Intel was churning in at high velocity and volumes, but there was still work to be done, particularly on the terrestrial front. A Real Time Regional Gateway (RTRG) data center and analytical hub was being considered and design options being formulated.

Todays brief was an informational brief, not decisional, and it was a rehearsal to brief ELIXER to higher offices in NSA. Still, it was another long day when Jon left the office for his drive home. He turned on his Sirius sat radio, changed the channel from Sirius Blues radio just in time to hear a reporter breathlessly announce that the US had killed by drone strike the principal military strategist and tactician in Iran's effort to deter Western influence and promote the expansion of Shiite and Iranian influence throughout the Middle East—Qasem Soleimani.

Chapter 20

January 5, 2020, Manda Bay

A troop of baboons clustered in the mango grove alongside the shore near the airfield were screaming. This early morning, they had good reason to raise the alarm-- RPGs had shattered the quiet dawn with violent explosions that rocked the small Kenyan naval base. What could only be al-Shabab militants had fired upon and destroyed a taxying De Havilland Dash-8.

Of the 4 Americans killed in the assault, 3 were contractors from L3 Technologies, the company to which Jon had been employed since 2013. Jon had never met these men but felt a kinship just the same. An Army soldier had also died in a firefight, and Jon grieved for him as well. It didn't really matter to him if the attack was or was not attributed to the Soleimani assassination. He still saw red, and he wanted retribution. Al Qaeda and its myriad of sick affiliates bring no value to the world, they only bring a twisted, distorted vision and misery, he thought.

Jon saw the backlash from the usual suspects such as Code Pink who gnashed their teeth over the legality of the GWOT in it's nearly second decade. He saw the politicians that either saw opportunity in an election year or those that tried to distance themselves from policy to have their political careers survive. He had always had some discontent with how policies came and went and sometimes questioned whether or not it made a whit of difference to any of the sacrifices Americans were making on a daily basis.

A feeling of helplessness crept stealthily in as it had right after 9/11. Where was I when the shit went down? Having a latte and watching some Netflix on my couch? He wrestled again with his old adversaries, depression and guilt. Feeling sorry for myself because I am 58 years old and retired from 30 years of service? Is that the excuse you want to play?

That was all interference and noise in the background to him as he made up his mind. The news was pretty much focused only on fatalities in the attack were covered at all rather than the trajectory of the stock market.

Through his own network Jon had learned the identities of those wounded at Manda Bay. One he knew quite well. 'Cuda had been shot in the leg and the GSW channeled deep in his flesh to touch his femoral artery. Were it not for the man from Ground Branch who had applied the single routing buckle tactical tourniquet, he would have bled out. 'Cuda was evacuated to DJ where he received freeze-dried plasma and initial surgery before being further evacuated to Doha to even better facilities enroute to Ramstein Air Base in Germany.

He picked up the phone and made the call.

Chapter 21

15 January 2020, Reston, VA

He had made his call, a call to the highest-ranking officer in CIA he had ever met, Glenn Gaffney, now retired. He made his request: pull strings, move mountains to get me on as an independent contractor forward deployed to either Kenya or Somalia – if there is to be a retaliatory strike, Jon wanted in. Gaffney had been in the S&T, but he also had been the number 3 maybe number 4 guy in the Agency. He had pull. The Agency always had the drone option as a possible course of action, so they deferred the likely decisive/CT direct action to DoD. However, the Agency did want a piece of the action as far as target development or close target recce. Since Jon had a working relationship with Jaylen who was the best boots on the ground operations officer in the AO, there was some logic in Jon joining a team, not to mention his SIGINT skills and familiarity with the Kenya/Somalia border area.

Jon also called LTG Mike Nagata (ret.) and asked for his running interference within DoD. Jon, a retired Army colonel, was asking to be an IC for what was highly probable to be a capture/kill mission, and he was asking to be part of an Agency team knowing there were elements in DoD that could do the job, one of which was the JRTF which Nagata had commanded. Nagata had been in the Ops squadron when Jon was on the JPO, so to a degree they knew each other. Jon was hoping the General could smooth ruffled feathers if JSOC planners wanted the entire mission serviced by DoD shooters and support elements. It was a very unconventional approach to call in these favors, but it was not completely unpalatable. The division of labor made some sense, and the teamwork between CIA and JSOC had been cemented over at least the last decade.

While Jon waited on pins and needles, he was thinking a secondary position would be to go for an extended TDY in Nairobi to bolster ELIXER construction in country. Parts of the system were active and been attributed by the Africa TOPI as having gathered tidbits of Iranian involvement with al Shabab, but no specifics. The trouble with electronic surveillance was if your adversary had discipline and stayed away from the phone or keyboard to a computer, no matter the expense, the systems would have nothing to find and sort and analyze into intelligence. The bottom line for him was, he was not going to sit this out.

Jon got the call, and to his surprise and elation which he tried not to show, the decision went his way. He would be placed on an access roster, report in to Camp Peary and on board as an IC at Redwood off Carter Creek road, then join the planning cell sequestered at Dogwood off Waller road. He was given instructions not to go into the Student Recreation Building (SRB) for any reason. Not really sure why he would, he thought. Planners from ST6 Gold Squadron, an hour's drive away, and paramilitary officers from Ground Branch (GB) met in the Dogwood conference center where they could SVTC secure video chat with the Special Warfare platoon commander in Manda Bay. The East Coast folks went to bed so they could adjust to Zulu time and get on the same sheet as the Manda Bay AFO team.

In the broadest strokes, the plan was to deploy the assaulters and the ISR/close recce assets to Nairobi for acclimation while greater target development efforts were focused to find those responsible for the attack; the on island SEALs at Manda Bay would continue with AFO activities and rehearse insertions in their indigenous fishing boats far south of prying eyes at the northern border of Kenya--- they would man the infil platform or emergency exfil platform if the target was along the coast (which was likely as one of the assaulters who had been wounded and interrogated assured his captors that he was indeed from a faction from Mogadishu, and there really is only one direct route).

More U-28 ISR birds would be prepositioned at Baledogle airfield where they were alerted to providing support, on order. Pred orbits from DJ would augment those from Baledogle when needed. The Directorate of Operations of CIA would provide, by name Jaylen Otis to exert influence on his network in support of the close recce team, on order. Aviation assets at Manda bay would support, either to assault or exfil, on order.

Not much more to plan until the target was found and fixed. Jon was on a separate flight out of BWI and a slightly different schedule offsetting the ST6 assaulters. He rode coach on Lufthansa; the SEALS flew business class on Qatar Airways. They were, after all, SEAL Team 6.

Chapter 22

22 February 2020, Somalia

The hard work of the Kenyan Defense Forces in AMISOM's Sector 2 uncovered, through rapport with the local villagers in Tabta, there was a group in a house on the west fringe of the village they suspected were foreign fighters. AFRICOM had drone surveillance over the target and began the process of establishing pattern of life of its occupants. It didn't take long to determine that the building was hosting a handful of malcontents from Shabab, and unfortunately the KDF commander decided to conduct a raid without prior coordination. The Shabab inhabitants fought back, most were killed, but two survived. Of those two survivors, during interrogation, one militant admitted not only being part of the attack on Manda Bay, but that the major planner of the attack was an Iranian, who went by Jamal Madan al-Tamini.

JSOC knew this man as Objective Dawa. OBJ Dawa had been on the JPEL for some time.

ELIXER had uncovered traces of IRGC-QF involvement in Somalia and Yemen over the last year. Snippets of conversations, whether coded in an elaborate nom de guerre schema or circuitous speech meant to obfuscate true meaning, it was clear Iran was deploying its extraterritorial forces to influence the Horn of Africa. With the uncovering of a single thread from an interrogation, the analysts with access to the PROTON database needed to conduct more intensive searches for hints of Dawa's presence. ELIXER was turning out to be a collection vacuum of epic proportions, with multiple ingests of 100 terabits per second, the problem then became sifting through the mundane to find the data that is truly meaningful. The Dawa thread gave them something on which to pull and they set new search parameters. What was needed was a location, not broad conspiracy theories.

Three were found. On the border at Ras Kamboni, at the large port town of Kismaayo, and at Baraawe just south of Mogadishu.

For the task force assembled at Manda Bay, the triplet of possibilities presented a small problem. The size of the ISR package couldn't cover all three towns, so it had to be augmented. Fortunately, the ST6 assaulter had brought two of their own intelligence operators from Black squadron, and the Stations at Nairobi and Dar as Salaam could pony up a technical operations officer each.

Jon flew into Manda Bay on the DIA C-12 from the embassy in Nairobi. On the tarmac, he was met with a booming, "Hey, Serp, remember me!!?"

"Young man, why yes I do," he replied, "but I have to go by Riptide now, 'cause some swine stole my call sign 'cause it was so cool." He extended his hand to the man who he knew as Jason Taylor, the Ground Branch operator who had applied the tourniquet to 'Cuda to save his life.

"Fair enough," the paramilitary officer offered, "I know you've been here before, but welcome to Manda Bay. I go by Xander, now. Wow, small world."

"Xander, I'd like to introduce Jaylen. He'll help us with

infrastructure," Riptide posited.

For those on the very pointy end of the spear, it was indeed a small world. Particularly with the physical extent of the range of operations of the GWOT, the 'G' in GWOT being Global and not hyperbole in the least. Coupled with the frequency over a duration of 18 years, those still around were bound to run across each other's path, the probability of such a small contingent of eligible warriors to conduct multiple, simultaneous operations dictated the intersects as very damn likely. The reunion would continue over beer if there was time, for now they had much to do.

Xander got Rip and Jaylen situated in billeting, a luxurious steel CONEX wet Chu with an AC and flat screen. Rip dumped his kit, and they went straight to the OPCEN.

Air planners mulled over maps and charts, calculated distances and relative airspeeds from Baledogle and DJ. Intel geeks made their requests for Predator FMV orbits on the Air Tasking Order (ATO) as did the S3 Air types for Close Air Support (CAS) sorties if required. Terrain analysts identified BLSs and HLZs for any conceivable contingency. The plan could be an assault from the sea or from a helicopter offset depending on which coastal town and where the target compound to be assaulted lie in relation to the sea. They just floated a myriad of courses of action while they waited for definition.

What was very clear is eyes on the ground would be necessary to confirm and fix Dawa's location.

The three R&S teams, imaginatively named RS 1, RS 2, and RS 3, huddled with the intel chief to determine their own plan for target development and to support an assault. RS 1, the Black squadron technical surveillance element took Baraawe; RS 2, Serpico and Xander, took Kismaayo; RS 3, the TOOs from Nairobi and Dar as Salaam, took Ras Kamboni. Teams 1 and 2 had a requirement to not only procure a safe house from which to operate, but also to procure both a Toyota Hilux type local indigenous truck in good working order and a warehouse in which to store it. Those warehouses would be stocked with extra cases of ammunition, med kits, grenades, and batteries.

Jaylen had many tricks up his sleeve; he had successfully recruited Abdi who had agreed to front some legitimate importing businesses in Mogadishu and Bossaso. This arrangement, even as a part-time proxy, gave Abdi a reason to travel to Somalia often, yet still have his domicile in the US where he could still live his American dream. Abdi was already in Kenya and could cross the border to procure two safe houses stocked with food, the Hilux and the warehouses in both Kismaayo and Mogadishu; the intel chief decided the vehicle contingencies were not necessary in Ras Kamoni as it was minutes from the border. Once these facilities were secured, two operators from the Manda Bay AFO SEAL platoon in low-vis vehicles would make the logistics run with a package to deposit in each warehouse, then return to base.

Loop had returned and taken over his old duties as HARC chief since 'Cuda had been injured. Loop had his safehouses secured in Ras Kamboni in less than a day. The TOOs took a meandering SDR and approached their observation post as safari vacationers from the Boni National Reserve.

While Abdi did his operational tasking, Serpico requested

refresher training with Xander. In his best Darth Vader voice, Xander intoned, "We meet again, at last. The circle is now complete. When I met you, I was but the learner. Now, I am the master."

"Yeah, yeah," Rip grimaced, "How about a nice road march. Just kidding, in all seriousness, I need to brush up on this MBITR comm gear. Sure, I know the basics of a software design radio, but I'll need to better understand the programmable cryptography for the AN/PRC-148 JEM. Also, some basic TTP like immediate action drills so we can flow as a team. I'm not talking CQB, just basic stuff. I could use going over the 9-lines protocol for medivac, close air support. Same with the transponders we might use to emplace navigational aids like beacons on an HLZ. I gotta know the SOPs so I am not a liability."

"I think we should take advantage of the facilities at Baledogle. Too many eyes here for me," Xander opined. "Some dispersal will not hurt, and we can infil overland from the west or north to attract less attention. I'll bounce a list of ideas off you, then think on a two-day POI so we can do rehearsals. I'll coordinate for Air, tell the chief our plan so he can rack and stack us on the appropriate ranges, while you pack all that gear to put on the bird."

Chapter 23

1 March 2020, Baledogle

The camp at Baledogle, compared to Manda Bay, was huge as it was a main training facility to AMISOM forces as well as an airbase for both drones and the COPPER DUNE U-28 aircraft fitted with EO and TYPHON GSM SIGINT cell tower emulators. Both airframes were run by DoD Air Force personnel assigned to the 16th Special Operations Wing. The small Agency contingent here had a CONEX of their own in the JSOC compound, but their business was purely HUMINT and they were targeting more strategic targets such as the President of Somalia, Mohamed Abdullahi Mohamed, who had publicly renounced his American citizenship but privately was on retainer to the CIA.

The senior ops NCO, a Senior Chief called Mojo, had secured ranges, transport and an unoccupied barracks office for Xander to use. The NCO served as the isolation facility, or ISOFAC. Mojo was to be considered an alternate in case either Xander or Riptide were indisposed; for the interim, he served as a LNO or Area Specialist Team (AST) conduit for any coordination back to Manda Bay. Additionally, Mojo loaned a Hilux that had been outfitted with pin hole cameras and other deep embed surveillance gear for use as the close recce vehicle. It was thin skinned, but it fit into the vibe of other Somali vehicles. The vehicle wouldn't stick out even if the occupants did.

The next day, Riptide and Xander both cycled through a labyrinth POI of round robin stations, not to create stress, but to fit in all the training necessary to polish Riptide's faded toolbox. Two hours were committed in the morning for classroom instruction on the VHF and SatCom radios they would carry in; they did some refresher IV training and Combat Zone Trauma Responder to focus on 'stopping the bleeding and keep them breathing', the proper application of Kerlix and an ACE wrap issued in their blow-out kits; they worked out SOPs as to who would set up a nav beacon and who would pull security, how they would cross linear danger areas if they had to patrol to reach a meeting site; Xander was a duly certified sniper with a surprisingly old school Remington 700 .300 Win Mag Rifle, Swarovski Z5i 25x scope and matching STS 80 20-60X Swarovski Optik spotting scope, the latter of which Riptide had to learn to effectively manipulate the eye relief.

The afternoons were dedicated to crawl, walk, run applications of the morning's classroom training in a field environment outdoors. Right after a lunch of sabaayad and dried meat with rice, they began their round robin with shooting, particularly fire and maneuver from cover to cover as a team. They cycled through each station, added a SOFLAM target designator station, then did it again until dinner. When it got dark, they cycled through the stations once more.

The next day, they added some fireman's carry sprints between stations and did it again, almost to midnight.

On the third day, they were called in to stop at the lunch break. Enough screwing around, infil is tonight, time to go to work. Mojo laid out the bones of the infil; Xander and Rip would drive their modified Hilux last in the order of march of a convoy of South African AMISON soldiers escorting a State Department dignitary in four Casspir armored personnel carriers to a meeting at Villa Somalia in Mogadishu; the Hilux would peel off at the outskirts of Garas Balley and proceed alone to Serendi, the compound where Halima had provided lodging and a place to link up with Abdi who would take over driving duties. Abdi would drive at night and Xander and Riptide would remain in the cab compartment with shemaghs to hide their whiteness.

It was too bad, once you got out of the cities of Mogadishu or even Baraawe, the countryside was beautiful. They would have seen many of the baobab species of trees, their distinctive silhouettes looming over the acacia scrubland, with Medusa-like branches spreading chaotically above a bulbous body. Some referred to their shape as being upside down, due to the root-like appearance of their entangled and twisted branches. Some referred to the baobab as the tree of life, as the trunk could retain hundreds of gallons of water in the dry climate. Planted firmly in the deep red soil of the low, rolling hills, it was a striking scene.

If it weren't dark, they also could have seen the infamous Mount Charcoal which had grown so massive because the UN Security Council imposed a ban on charcoal exports in 2011 to cut off Al Shabaab's revenues. Abdi was by now clearly on edge, as the stress of driving and carrying two foreigners in the cab section was fraying his nerves. Abdi did, however, remain intact and got them to the safe house in one piece. They offloaded the equipment quickly and quietly, got inside where Abdi nearly collapsed from exhaustion.

The three men were in Kismaayo, uncompromised and ready to go. Xander called it in on the Satphone, set the watch, and Adbi and Riptide bedded down. RS 2 was in place.

Chapter 24

05 1300Z MAR 20, Kismaayo

There were whispers. A phone call in Yemen asserted that the brothers there missed the guidance of Faleh Abu al-Shaabi. An IP address that resolved to an internet café in Syria from GHOSTHUNTER revealed content of contact with Jamal inquiring if travel plans to RK were all set. ELIXER played a role, but the NSA's net is widely cast and global in it's reach. RS 1 in Baraawe discovered two hives of activity and had sprouted an additional pair of Black squadron operators to cover the second Shabab compound. A defector in the Serendi house surrendered a flip phone with an SMS detailing al-Shaabi's transmission output shaft gasket failure on the blue Suzuki Escudo. That phone was ripped with forensics software to gather pertinent selectors such as IMEIs and IMSIs. Preds searched the roadways for a blue Suzuki.

Riptide had set up his gear and was finding little signal strength from any position inside their safe house. It caused him considerable concern as he and Xander were limited to only sporadic forays in the Hilux at night, even though they wore concealing clothing and disguises that were specially fabricated latex masks with darker pigmentation. G squadron of Delta had perfected these masks, but they only worked in passing—they would not hold up to scrutiny in a personal encounter with any Somali, not to mention neither one of them spoke the language.

Rip asked Abdi to take a spin around where he had a vector

of decent signal strength and where he made a guess on the map of from where it may emanate. He rehearsed a map recon of the route with Abdi who, when done, would continue to his import business in Mogadishu as a cover for action, then went over the procedures of how to operate the concealed pinhole cameras, and sent him on his way. The whole cycle would take the remainder of the day and tomorrow.

When Abdi returned and the data from the SD card was downloaded and reviewed, a single frame showed promise:

Clearly, at the base of the tower on the right, the parabolic dishes for an Abis interface were visible. The deep install camera had an integrated GPS, which Rip plotted. Right smack in the middle of town near the Northern Industrial Center. Since their second safe house was in the Shaqaalaha District in the west part of town and even less advantageous line of sight position, RS 2 reported into base with a request to move to the warehouse site near the abandoned meat packing factory. Not only would that have better fidelity for signals, but it was less densely populated as the residential area they were currently staged.

That night, Adbi drove the Hilux with Riptide twisting knobs and conducting a survey from the back cab under a blanket. The survey showed a much improved signal environment near the warehouse. Riptide reported this back to Manda Bay and received a go to displace. They all bedded down for the night to prepare for the next day's move and occupation of the warehouse where Abdi had stored not a Hilux, but a disheveled looking silver Nissan Xterra and the assorted stores.

The next day they broke down and sterilized the patrol base in which they had been mostly sequestered for nearly three weeks; that was a pretty long time, they really need to move anyway. Abdi took one load of surveillance kit buried underneath all their food and water in the afternoon with the on-board cameras running. The more sensitive gear to include the .300 Win Mag and all their other fighting gear and radios was loaded up after dark and they all three jammed in and set out for the 6 kilometer SDR to the warehouse with Xander calling out the turns from the back seat.

At the new site and foregoing a leader's recon, they quietly occupied the site by force where after a security sweep, Xander inspected the vehicles and stores while Rip set up all the surveillance and commo gear. Since getting intel from the BACKTRACK receiver was their raison d'etre at this point, other priorities of work were set aside, yet Xander still set the watch. Riptide set up the Satcom and oriented his antenna to the point on the horizon where there was a bird in RLOS and reported in that they were set.

At the comm shack in the Manda Bay OPCEN, Loop came back, "RS 2, be advised that overhead had spotted a blue Suzuki Escudo driving south of RS 1's position late afternoon and dropped the vehicle follow in the clutter entering your location vicinity HLZ 1." Loop was referring to previously determined grid reference graphic (GRG) points that had been set from satellite photos. There was a much smaller possible HLZ 2 on a football pitch just south of the Government Quarters, but HLZ 1 was the Kismaayo Stadium right across from the bus station, which Xander had confirmed as having no vertical obstacles in one of the area fam patrols.

The game was afoot, indeed.

Chapter 25

26 1300Z MAR 20, Kismaayo

"I assume you recall some of the advantages and disadvantages of the A-bis interface, young padawan?", Rip tossed to Xander.

"Got me," Xander admitted ruefully. "It's a little fuzzy. My wife was the one into that shit."

Rip continued his lecture to his enamored partner in crime, "Short story, we'll get some location fidelity, but no call content, i.e., conversation."

Xander nodded. "We'll still have to get PID eyes on to confirm the hit."

"True dat. But we can continue to refine with the TYPHON once we get a lock," Rip explained, "If he's active, we'll be able to neck it down. Since the initial data was off of SMS messaging, it's reasonable he's not on talking long anyway. We'll only have a few shots before he tosses the burner anyway."

It turned out the RS 2 ground-based collector missed the SMS, but the overhead U-28 with APG didn't. Touchdown. The cell phone emitter was determined to be in the area framed by a roughly triangle shape of roads between the north and south industrial centers. Within that wedge of built up area, 90% of Kismaayo's best hotels were clustered.

Loop had called in and relayed the data. Abdi would go solo, again, and drive around and look for the blue Suzuki. He was gone only a short time. When he returned, his excitement was readily apparent.

"I found it!" he exclaimed. Abdi was earning his paycheck and his participation was far beyond his wildest imagination. Although he loved his new life in America, he also wanted to rid his native-born Somalia of this scourge called al-Shabaab.

Abdi was still flush, and he continued in his high-pitched voice, "The car was just outside the Tawakal Hotel. I have it all on the camera."

Very carefully, Riptide went through the footage and sure enough, there it was. He isolated a few frames and transferred them to the laptop. At this point he handed the task over to Xander as his familiarity with sending data over the PRC-155 radio with the MUOS High Power Amplifier (MHPA) attached was not worth the risk of losing the file. He was OK operating it on voice, and his pre-deployment training had focused on inter-team comms over the MBITR.

Xander took charge, all business. This is why we are here, he thought. Provide eyes on to assist the assault, both in developing plans and running contingencies on the ground. File uploaded and sent, he replied laconically, "All too easy."

With an initial location, the assaulters could plan in earnest. Since OBJ Dawa was a commander in the IRGC-QF, he had far greater value alive than dead. That was their mindset as they formulated their plan. This was not just some low-level facilitator Taliban bubba like you might find and kill on the border of Pakistan, this could be a strategic acquisition. The key was stealth and speed. Violence of action would come naturally if it hit the fan, be assured. They started with the assumption that Dawa was at or near the Tawakal Hotel, less than half a click from the low water mark of the bay at Qoryoley Beach. Steam the indig fishing boats close enough to shore to swim the last 500 meters pulling tethers attached to flotation devices with the heavy gear; HAHO jump off shore to get close enough to the beach to land in the water, then complete the same swim evolution to dry land. Assemble, gear up. Link up with RS 2 at Beach Landing Site (BLS), patrol to target area. Recce. Assault. Exfil could be fast RHIBs with specially designed acoustic dampened cowlings to muffle engines at a secondary BLS on Leedo Beach or TBD. Alternatively, exfil could be l/u with RS 2 trucks, ground route to HLZ 1 with 23 PAX, sling load specially modded Hilux, or blow in place to destroy sensitive gear on board the Hilux.

And so on the ideation of a working CONOP to capture/kill Objective Dawa. In rapid succession, courses of action would be discarded or evaluated in detail. For Riptide, Xander and Abdi, their part was certain. They would, on order, occupy the abandoned Asasey Hotel to establish overwatch. The hotel had been destroyed by a car bomb the year prior and there was no money or will to rebuild. However, its hulking skeleton offered concealment and it was only a block away from the Tawakal Hotel, noted as Bld 45 and Bld 48 on the GRG, respectively. They could use the vehicle TYPHON for an additional sensor, but the Pred with GILGAMESH was on orbit 15,000 feet overhead. RS 2 would also mark BLS 1 with IR strobes, just in case, and be prepared to (BPT) mark BLS 2 and HLZ 2.

RS 3 would join the KDF quick reaction force (QRF) on the Kenyan border. R2 1 would leave Baraawe with their vehicles, pause and hole up at the bus station across from the stadium

(HLZ 1) which they would mark with IR strobes and nav beacon. RS 1 would then augment the RS 2 vehicles to pick up the remainder of the assault team. The convoy would then speed to HLZ 1 or the BLS for exfil. Clearly, the long pole in the tent was timing. Once the action was called, all command and control went to Casper, the Gold squadron platoon commander.

Once again, RS 2 displaced and took up their new positions on the Asasey Hotel roof or fourth floor windows. First order of business was setting up a hide site in which Xander and Riptide could place the long gun and more importantly, the optics on tripods. The Swarovski spotting scope allowed an adapter on which a digital camera could be attached. Riptide took several pictures; although they would not be able to do a 360 panoramic around the Tawakal, this was good for planning the approach to the front of the building. In what may have been the most surprising act of initiative ever, Abdi loitered in the lobby and over heard the desk clerk, followed his intuition as to what he heard, took the elevator to the third floor and peaked down the hall to see what could only be two guards posted on the flanks of door 327 by his count. Certainly, it was the street side of the building on the third deck.

Riptide was completely aghast, but overjoyed with the information, but cautioned, "OK, Abdi, well done, well done, indeed. Let's throttle back for a tad. I can't wait to talk to Jaylen! One way or another, we'll get you home in one piece. Now, I gotta get this data out."

"I got it from here," Xander said, "I'll shoot this out, then I'll break down the SATCOM link. This is going to go fast now, we're on voice and more likely just on the handheld."

Riptide concurred and put Abdi down for a few winks. Abdi had already parked the Xterra nearby, so there was nothing to do but try to rest. On the roof, Xander played with the comm gear, hit send and waited. He listened on the headphones as he sighted through the rifle scope. He swept the third floor until he could see movement in the windows. In what could only be 327, an olive skinned man with an extremely manicured beard sat at the desk sipping a glass of water. Xander, thought, well that guy looks about as Persian as I can figure. He made one last call on the SATCOM telling base eyes on, PID.

The Gold commander made his decision and relayed the timings to RS 1 and RS 2. RS 1 would SP NLT 1800Z, be in position at the bus station NLT 0001Z having set the IR strobe and navigation beacon mid field, near recognition safe signal - red chemlight; Gold would jump HAHO, link up at BLS 1 approximately 2300Z; RS2 set IR strobe at BLS 1 to signal team in, then guide assaulters to Hotel H, near recognition signal – blue chemlight; R2 would overwatch and report on channel 6, link up with Gold on order and pick up/drive to HLZ 1 for l/u with RS 1, headcount and extraction.

Xander back briefed rip and Abdi. Once again, Abdi did the extraordinary – quite casually he said, "I will take the Hilux with me to my import business shop in Mogadishu. Hanging it underneath a helicopter sounds bad and may take time."

Xander looked at Rip with dismay and said, "Only if it is calm, Abdi. Otherwise, we are taking you with us. Deal?"

Riptide added, "In case you aren't getting enough action, I would like you to be the receiving party down at the beach at 11:00 pm. The street that the hotel is on runs straight to the beach, so I don't see them having a difficult time finding it, but that is the plan. Can you do this for us, Abdi?"

Abdi smiled, "Of course, Mr. Rip. Just show me what to do."

Chapter 26

27 0001Z MAR 20, Actions on the objective

From their perch on the roof of the crumbling Asasey Hotel, Rip and Xander could plainly see Abdi and the SEAL platoon flitting amongst the shadows on the street leading from the quay. It was 3:00 am; there was no one else out and about to witness the stealth and appreciate the choreography of men quietly advancing in a dance of bounding overwatch. After nearly 20 years of combat, an offset infil nearly always trumped the flare right over the 'X' and fast rope onto the objective method. For a snatch operation, there was no better alternative.

A group of two wearing the latex disguises and clad in dark hued macawiis, khameez and the embroidered caps called a koofiyad proceeded the main body, presumably to neutralize the front desk clerk and gain initial entry. The fact they had AK-47s in this country would raise no alarm; the silenced pistols might. They were closely followed by assaulters bounding in black kit by groups of four who immediately made for the stairs on the northern most wall. Other assaulters took defensive positions outside and stayed out of sight if they could still maintain their fields of fire.

The radio was silent, not a word spoken. The recon team saw two flashes of bright light illuminate what they believed to be room 327; not a sound, no blasts of a self-detonated suicide vest, no bullets rending the still of the deep, black night.

"All hands, assemble at Cache 2 for pick up, 4 mikes," Casper keyed his radio on channel 6.

Rip and Xander snatched up the rifle, the tripods, the spotting scope, the camo netting under which they had lain, and each got to their assigned Hilux and Xterra respectively. Two minutes later the other two RS 1 vehicles loitered in the rally point. In less than a minute, the main body of the Gold squadron assaulters found the transports, loaded up in prearranged chalks, and the convoy sped off to HLZ 1.

Three sterilized trucks were abandoned in the bus station parking lot and would likely be stolen by morning; it didn't matter, they had served their purpose. Abdi, who had even remembered to police up the IR strobe with which he had signaled the SEAL platoon at the BLS, drove off to Mogadishu, alone and, apparently, unafraid.

Casper tapped each man in as they filed by. 22 PAX, split into two chalks onto the two CH-47s, no sling load. The helicopters' TOT was less than a minute, and one after the other lifted vertically above the stadium walls and they were off to Manda Bay in what could have been the most anticlimactical operation in recent history. "Few shots fired, 2 EKIA, no American casualties, 3 Touchdowns (2 cell phone, 1 laptop), and hugely successful relative to payload: Objective DAWA, aka Jamal Madan al-Tamimi, aka Faleh Abu al-Shaabi had been detained and would soon come to understand the proverb "revenge is a dish best served cold."

Chapter 27
July 11, 2020 Epilogue

Jon Prescott sat on his couch in his townhouse in Laurel, sipping a brew of chai tea and thinking about a great many things as he was inclined to do lately. Still on work sabbatical, he enjoyed getting up later than 8:00 am and staying up late to eat popcorn and watching a streamed movie until he felt like it. He was restful, yet restless.

His thoughts went to Kismaayo, and lately, particularly of Abdi. If there were a hero in this story, it was Abdi. Jon thought, this young man from Maine had *left* that war weary husk of a country called Somalia and had come to these United States of America to pursue the dream of happiness, security, and hope. Hope found in that that he could live a simple life on 'a farm with a barn, a horse, chickens and guinea hens.' It is very hard to know the percentages, the distribution of those who have come and labored to assimilate fully into a new American life, but Jon believed Abdi to be the poster child, a pilgrim that came to these shores with the gift of acceptance and humility.

In the flight to base, Jon had leaned over to Casper and requested the Gold team leader relay to Mojo that a Pred and the AC-130 should cover Abdi's drive to Mogadishu. It should be an easy vehicle follow; Jon had placed a one inch square of glint tape on the roof of the Hilux. Mojo would eventually make arrangements for an APC convoy to escort the Hilux back to Baledogle; Abdi's service in the operation was complete.

Jon looked back over the course of the past twenty years and could not recall any soldier he knew that was as brave and selfless as Abdi. That in itself says a lot; he had worked with great Americans for two decades who directly or indirectly toiled in the GWOT, some of whom were highly decorated for valor. But in the balance, to say that Abdi went above and beyond his call to duty would not even come close to expressing the level to which he rose in the service of his Country.

Jon chuckled to himself in his reminisces. He recalled being a young, Infantry second lieutenant far across the Chattahoochee at Ft. Benning's School for Boys. He had been pumping gas at the AAFES Shopette, in uniform with no hat. A gravelly voice call rang out, "Where's your fucking cover, LT?"

Jon turned round, and across the pump station was an older man, wearing a wide blue ribbon with thirteen white stars, under which was suspended a bronze colored star shaped medal, what he recognized too late as the Medal of Honor. The man had clearly been an ass kicking NCO and he exclaimed, "Don't you dumb ass lieutenants have enough sense to salute a guy wearing this! Lock your fucking heels and get your head out of your fourth point of contact, Airborne!" The ass chewing, resplendent in its magnificent use of profane superlatives, ended as abruptly as it began when that old vet gloriously drove away in his '67 boattail 'Vette.

No doubt that gentleman had deserved the MOH, none at all, but Jon thought this civilian called Abdi was likely in the same league. He had been recruited to return to a hellhole and rent apartments, yet he performed well above his brief, performed with no complaint, alone in an environment that was swimming with insurgents and a road block around any bend. He did this to bring justice to a sociopath about whom he knew nothing. He had placed his faith on the levers of government who oversaw the rollback of tyranny; he had placed his faith in America because he believed that America was that 'shining city on the hill'.

He spent the rest of the morning digging into some reading. The Internet was such a wonderful resource. The New York Times headline read, "**Defying U.S., China and Iran Near Trade and Military Partnership**". To him, and anyone else involved in ELIXER, this was not a shocker at all. The article pontificated, "The partnership, detailed in an 18-page proposed agreement obtained by The New York Times, would vastly expand Chinese presence in banking, telecommunications, ports, railways and dozens of other projects. In exchange, China would receive a regular — and, according to an Iranian official and an oil trader, heavily discounted — supply of Iranian oil over the next 25 years."

Jon had served in uniform from Reagan to Obama, loyally riding the peaks and troughs of the sinusoidal wave of policy fluctuations with seemingly little common ground. Gone were the days when Democrats and Republicans could at least agree that the Soviet Union was bad, Communism was bad, and that America stood the ramparts of all that is good and just. There were still a few true Patriots, and in their ranks were

149 men and women like Abdi, Jill Monroe, Rachel and Dan 'Xander' Howard, Jaylen, Mojo, Loop and 'Cuda.

Jon had applied the balm of relief to his past angst by doing his part. He was, at last, to at least a larger degree content. He thought, now what the hell am I gonna do?

At that moment, his phone rang.

Made in the USA
Monee, IL
14 January 2022